TO DIE
IN
New York

LOUIS WIGDORSKY VOGELSANG

authorHOUSE®

AuthorHouse™
1663 Liberty Drive
Bloomington, IN 47403
www.authorhouse.com
Phone: 1 (800) 839-8640

Published by AuthorHouse 03/22/2018

ISBN: 978-1-5462-3488-3 (sc)
ISBN: 978-1-5462-3487-6 (hc)
ISBN: 978-1-5462-3486-9 (e)

Library of Congress Control Number: 2018903653

Print information available on the last page.

Fortunately, the events narrated in this novel are highly unlikely but, unfortunately, entirely possible. Humanity has an extremely high potential for stupidity and irrationality.

Luis Wigdorsky Vogelsang

With affection for my parents, Victor Wigdorsky and Marta Vogelsang, who have cared for me for so many years from far, far above the sun and stars.

Some time ago, the following prayer came to me:

My beloved Lord, I know that I am a sinner, but I have the desire to turn away from my sins and surrender my life to You. I ask for your forgiveness and mercy so you will enter my heart and guide my life and be my personal Lord and Savior. Thank you for saving me. In the name of Jesus, amen.

The truth is that I didn't believe him. He was begging because of fear, because of despair; he was lying to me so things might go well for him in the worldly lie.

I, HE WHO IS

Acknowledgements

Before anyone else, I give thanks to God who gave me the desire and the sensitivity to read fiction and the enjoyment of writing about imaginary worlds.

I also thank my dear friends Rodrigo Ramírez Dellepiane and Patricio Ramírez Vásquez for generously publishing my first book of short stories *Un tren al Paraíso y otros cuentos de Carabineros* and for encouraging me to continue writing fiction.

I give my gratitude to Carmela Altamura and Leonard Altamura, both good American friends, for giving me a place to stay for six months in New Jersey, where I was able to finish this novel by experiencing the atmosphere of New York in person.

María Inés Bravo, my ex-wife, who encouraged me by reading the first manuscript. I offer her my most sincere thanks for her support, as always.

Finally, my family remains in my heart. My wife Eliana Amunátegui and my children Luis, Víctor and Joshua. Without the understanding of all of them, the peaceful atmosphere that they create around me and their tolerance of my madness to continue acting like a child when playing with fiction, it would never have been possible for me to write this novel or any of those I will write in the future.

Chapter 1

W e began to realize that the old, old man, Plaza de los Reyes, was crazy when we heard him say that the only thing he wanted in what remained of his life, condemned by cancer of the colon, was to die in New York. He also said that he wouldn't buy a plane ticket to fly there, but would travel by air as a stowaway on the first plane he could sneak onto, just like in the American movies. He only knew the United States of America through the movies and since his childhood he had always wanted to be Superman or Clark Gable or John Wayne, beating the bad guys with bullets in the Far West or fighting for the free world as a soldier in war movies. Sometimes he dreamed he was Fred Astaire, gliding alongside Ginger Rogers on shiny black floors gleaming like mirrors to the music of Gershwin or Cole Porter. The eccentricities of multimillionaires are far from uncommon and dreams are inevitable in the minds of ordinary people.

My wife Antonieta and I knew that Fernandísimo Plaza de los Reyes, that distinguished old man with the air of a baron or Asturian count, was a fanatic, a blind and passionate lover of the United States, but we couldn't explain why he wanted to die in New York and far less why he would have to fly there as a stowaway, knowing he was a millionaire bachelor and that he didn't have anyone even close who he could leave as his heir. It was an eccentricity that was hard to understand.

The truth is that Antonieta and I could call ourselves the closest people to him and that was why each of us cozied up to him, and in the most secret, complicit silence, to become, as God would surely want to be us to be someday, his absolute heirs. His fortune lay, to put it one way, like a gigantic mountain of gold ingots buried deep beneath the ground, supporting the huge, majestic and castle-like mansion in which he dwelt, a silent hermit, like Dracula removed from the worldly fuss of blood.

Someday those ingots would be bills, green dollar bills in my eager pockets. I should confess, even to myself, that the feeling I could possibly be an heir of Plaza de los Reyes was a secret kept in my heart very much under lock and key, which not even Antonieta could suspect. In turn, I had the suspicion that she harbored the very same hope as best she could from me. But I was always convinced that Antonieta suspected the same of me. Each of us no doubt supposed the existence of that secret in the dark recesses of the other's mind. But we kept quiet and when our eyes met, we simply smiled and said nice things or danced tango, rock or very sexy cumbias, or bathed naked in the lake. I sensed that Antonieta didn't share her intimate desire with me for the same reasons that I didn't share my secret with her. It was a question of money and a lot of it, perhaps too much. And although it doesn't cost much to share a one-thousand or two-thousand peso bill, sharing a huge fortune hurts. Wealth is harder to share than poverty. When he died, and if he had the intention of leaving his wealth, he would do so thinking of Antonieta and myself. "I will leave my fortune to that marvelous couple that has come to be like my family," the rich Fernandísimo Plaza de los Reyes would almost certainly think or say. And that was what neither she nor I liked –to share– and so we said nothing to each other. Although it may seem a contradiction, there is evidence that is not manifest but remains like unequivocal latencies very deep within our intuitions.

There's also another issue in this internal intrigue. It's all or nothing. If we both inherited the fortune of Plaza de los Reyes, I'm very certain and, indeed, absolutely convinced, that she would murder me to keep everything for herself or I would kill her for the same motives. Now, let's be clear. Antonieta and I are husband and wife by both civil and church law, we make love like crazy teenagers, we practice all the sexual positions of the Kama Sutra plus a few others we have created ourselves and we've even been occasional swingers, and we love each other dearly. But in this life, as things are, as circumstances occur, there are some matters that fade into the background. Moreover, either facing the civil official or before the priest in the church, nobody told us that we had to put love before money. When things aren't explained clearly and in detail, one is free to interpret them as one chooses.

Her name is Antonieta Gellini del Pozo and I'm Ricardo Pozo Almendras. This is just in case we appear in the papers.

Chapter 2

I f one doesn't want to arrive to visit a friend in the nude, the most reasonable thing to do is to never leave towels and clothes on the shore of a lake and bathe in its water as God cast you into the world. On Sundays we used to go swimming in the lake with Antonieta and that particular Sunday was no different to any of the previous ones during the summer. There was a hellish heat and we frolicked naked in the cool, crystalline water, like two young sea lions in love. "You've got a terrific ass, you're making me nervous," and she responded with a laugh, unchecked like hair in the wind, and between the peals of laughter she pretended to be shocked with a dirty "that thing between your legs has got big and hard." "All the better to eat you with, my dear," and she swam away crying "help, help the wolf is coming and I'm little Red Riding Hood." I started swimming after her, but I was too aroused and couldn't paddle fast enough to catch her. From afar, Antonieta yelled "if you catch me, you can do what you want with me" and floating on her back she stroked her breasts and licked her lips lustfully with that tasty tongue that I had felt inside my mouth countless times. "Don't be cruel," I shouted, "you come over here, I can't reach you there, my arms can't take it. Come on, don't be unkind, you'll force me to jerk off right here." She laughed again and gave me permission, "go on then, I'll watch you." So I started to do so, standing on the lake bed with the water up to my neck and Antonieta began doing the same, and while we did that we looked at each other over the distance, putting on depraved faces and yelling out erotic and pornographic swearwords until, at the peak of our ecstasy, we shared a final explosion of pleasure. An immense aquatic orgasm. Then there was the silence of the landscape and the twittering of birds.

— Let's get to the shore, it's time to go. Let's get our clothes and get dressed

— Shit, the clothes are gone, Antonieta!

— That can't be. Look for them, maybe we didn't leave them here. Behind the bushes.

— ...nothing behind the bushes.

— Ricardo, no for God's sake... Up on the branch of the tree.

— ... nothing, nothing here and nothing there. Antonieta, someone has stolen our clothes and even the towels!

— That's what we get for living in this shitty country! It's full of thieves, from those at the top to the even the lowest of the low! No wonder Fernandísimo wants to go and live in New York and die there! If they bury him here in little old Chile, they might even desecrate his grave to steal everything!

When I realized, I understood that Antonieta was quite right in what she said. In Chile there was a red carpet rolled out for criminals.

— Damn it, Antonieta, the car!

— Ricardo, no, not the car, for God's sake! And us naked!

Chapter 3

I know what everyone thinks and feels and that's why, without ever having opened my mouth, I know that Ricardo Pozo Almendras is very wrong about Fernandísimo Plaza de los Reyes. The same is true of the identical expectations of his wife, Antonieta Gellini del Pozo. Both of them are perfectly false and hypocritical. But of course, they love each other, they love each other dearly. Well, obviously, that's what those who populate the Earth as the dominant species call Love. They love each other so much that she has already decided more or less how to murder her husband when the time comes, when, according to their ridiculous pretensions, Fernandísimo Plaza de los Reyes will leave his huge fortune to the couple. She has been thinking of poison; maybe strychnine or cyanide. The problem is that it's not easy to get those substances and if they are obtained the evidence of the purchase remains for the police to investigate. And of course the police would investigate, as death by poisoning is notorious and would require an autopsy, a medical-legal study and then little Antonieta would be in serious trouble and could well finish her inheritance behind bars. There was something else that troubled Antonieta. She would like Ricardo to have a painless death, a merciful, sweet death, like a baby falling asleep in its cradle. But what lethal substance could cause such a death? There was no mistaking it, Antonieta loves Ricardo with all her heart. Something similar goes for the absurd intentions of her loving husband Ricardo. He has already pretty much decided on the modus operandi to assassinate his sweet and fiery Antonieta. Ricardo is a man who watches a lot of cinema and particularly likes gangster movies, especially if they are about Al Capone and star Edward G. Robinson. He has seen The Godfather exactly seventy-one and a half times, since the last time he had to interrupt his evening to take part in another absolutely unforeseen eventuality for him. Antonieta unexpectedly arrived in the bedroom with a young guy of athletic build whom she had picked up in the street and who was willing to participate in a ménage à trois with them. The Godfather continued his development alone and abandoned on the TV screen while the three of them happily and nakedly dedicated themselves to humping as many times as possible. But, in the end, the important thing is to know that his love of cinema led him to conceive of murdering his wife with a contract killing. He would hire a hitman and her would shoot her, pretending it was a robbery, or he would kidnap her and then drown her in the sea or in some aquatic area that had as much water as possible. The problem is that the hitman would have that information and could extort him at any time by constantly asking for money for a lifetime or, even worse, demanding a stratospheric sum for his silence. That would force him to hire another hitman to eliminate the first one, but then the latter would do the same and everything would be reduced to a chain of crimes in order to conceal the original one. He would become a real Macbeth, but Ricardo never had a theatrical vocation and besides, aside from the stress, the economic cost wouldn't be worth it. The cost-benefit balance was tipped more toward cost than benefit. You didn't have to be a Wall Street financier to realize that. In this case, it was better for him to leave the woman of his dreams alive and share the inheritance with her, which was in keeping with both the law and good manners. But the law and good manners had never been very appealing to either of them and anyway, that wasn't the idea. The idea was all or nothing. He would have to think of something else that would be as close as possible to the perfect crime. To be fair –I can't stop being that way because I'd stop being me– Ricardo also loves his wife. It's just that his love isn't as compassionate, as merciful as that of Antonieta. Her suffering when dying was of little consequence to him. In the end, he thought, if Antonieta came into the world suffering (birth is a pain, she always said), why she couldn't she leave this world in pain. In the end, he reflected, death should be a quick, instantaneous pain of millionths of a second and then nothing; rest or perhaps another life, or maybe heaven or maybe hell. But all of that was already out of reach. He could answer for everything until the moment of the final death rattle and after that his pockets would be bulging with cash for him and him alone.

In their homo sapiens heads these thoughts, plans and intentions were churning day and night and even when deeply asleep they appeared in the form of terrifying nightmares in which the other's corpse persecuted the murderous spouse and the image of the cadaver never ceased having thick rivulets of blood spurting from torn skin and flesh and green substances spewing from the eye sockets and other bodily cavities. They were Hollywood-like nightmares in the purest horror movie style.

It was all an immense and useless expenditure of energy. It was a lamentable waste of time, glucose and phosphorus because, to tell the truth, what they should have been thinking about was the last thing they would have imagined: Mr. Bob.

This individual, of a robust build but calm temper, remained somewhat in the shadows and deep within the heart of Fernandísimo Plaza de los Reyes. He loved him dearly and although he never spoke to him when he was with other friends, leaving him alone in total silence despite his presence, in the wanderings of his mind he had already had hints of the idea of leaving him his entire inheritance. Mr. Bob could never have suspected it and even if he had, his disinterested nature would have left him undaunted. He, Mr. Bob, wasn't made to enjoy that kind of fortune. No, definitely, not at all. He belonged to a superior lineage, a kind of aristocracy in which wealth had nothing to do with money or any such pursuits. That said, Fernandísimo would never state this hidden intention, which emerged almost at the level of his conscience, to anyone for anything in the world and even less so to Mr. Bob. Mr. Bob was English and although he wasn't American (Fernandísimo adored Americans) he was definitely his best friend. He preferred to speak to him in English (thus practicing the language) when they were alone when the long hours of talk turned to the human and the divine and the sad and decadent human condition. The history of humanity is the story of infamy and hypocrisy, he would say to him, a story forged with blood and fire, destruction and submission, slavery and torture of all kinds; corporal, psychological, social, political. It is the story of man, being at every moment the wolf to man. Here, Fernandísimo reaffirmed, in this fucking history of humanity, there are no red riding hoods, only wolves and nothing but wolves. With his silence Mr. Bob always seemed to agree, never contradicting him. It appeared that he was always, always in complete agreement with his millionaire friend. Well then, that would be the grotesque end of the ambitious and foul pretensions of the married lovers who planned to murder each other once allocated the inheritance they were sure to receive from Fernandísimo Plaza de los Reyes. To be fair to them, because justice is mine, it was understandable that they failed to consider the stumbling block that Mr. Bob represented to their anxious desires, not that they were naïve or foolish in that sense. Life experience gives people a certain logic to understand and interpret reality, a minimum common sense with regard to causes and effects as to what is possible and what is not, what can be expected to happen and what not. It was therefore perfectly and understandably impossible for them to imagine that Fernandísimo Plaza de los Reyes had any serious intention of leaving his entire fortune to a dog, to Mr. Bob.

Chapter 4

It was very clear to me that the madness that Antonieta and I supposed was dwelling inside the noble and gray head of Fernandísimo Plaza de los Reyes wasn't that he wanted to die in New York. Everyone is free to choose the place where they want their bones to be buried and opting not to be in the ground of a country you detest is perfectly understandable and, moreover, is a logical, normal, consistent and even plausible decision. Well, plausible as long as the funeral costs aren't much higher than in the country you hate. In such a case, it's more understandable and normal to put aside certain nitpicking, to pretend to be a patriot, remain in your country and reserve a grave in some cemetery, checking the best price in the funeral market. Money is no laughing matter and you have to put it where it's deserved. In the case of Fernandísimo Plaza de los Reyes, who has much more than a few pennies to rub together, it wouldn't be a question of avarice, but rather a matter of knowing how to move smartly and wisely in a free market society with much more liberal consumption. And it is precisely in that and one or two other details in which I consider the madness of our friend and, I hope, future benefactor to lie. A funeral in New York is, I imagine, a thousand times more expensive than in Chile, but Fernandísimo insists on his idea, almost rudely overriding all norms, directives, practices and doctrines of the economic sciences. To be a good Samaritan in current times and in societies that are lucky enough not to be ruled by the Islamic State, is so much more bizarre than being one in biblical times, when at least the tangible presence of Jesus Christ walking the earth made it understandable and natural to want to be generous and philanthropic, even to the detriment of one's own bag of coins. One must consider that when Jesus was alive and, in case of any doubts about what he may have said or in light of any whimsical interpretation of his words, there was the possibility of going to clarify things with him personally, face to face and, if the meeting was after a meal, with at least three toasts with a full cup, perhaps even side by side. Therefore, if a person decided to become a good Samaritan or chose to shun the material goods of this Earth, it didn't attract quite so much attention and if he aroused suspicions and gossip about possibly being crazy, he had an advocate at hand to defend him, the Lord Jesus himself. Nowadays, on the other hand, he's no longer active and present among us. We're left with the Holy Scriptures of his teachings, but the word of mouth has diverged a long way from the original source, or the written word has no solid or objective support and lends itself to any idiot or wise man's apprentice distorting its tone to their own ends or interpreting it as they wish. Who told you that the one who said what he said really existed? And how do you know that what he meant by what he said is what you believe? And how do you know whether the one who said what he said was a madman and whether his reasons were nothing but the reasons of the unreasonable? Stop the nonsense and go, enjoy, consume, take good care of your money and make it productive! Opting for wastefulness motivated by cravings and considerations that we cannot see or touch, as in the case of Fernandísimo bent on dying in New York despite the costliness of the idea, is obviously crazy in any light nowadays. He should realize that today there are other gospels, concrete ones, with authors who are still alive or, if not, who are not long gone and which have been proven to work by motivating, mobilizing and exalting the multitudes who are prompted by their purchasing power or their enormous potential for indebtedness, and that indebtedness is power, the possibility to decide on the source of pleasures, the wellbeing of the flesh and bones that we see in the mirror each day. They are the gospels of an Adam Smith, a Keynes, a Rockefeller and even a Donald Trump, and the sacred temple is no longer a ruined building solely of interest to archeologists like the Temple of King Solomon. No, they're solid, tall and existing buildings on the iconic Wall Street, a stone's throw from the bull that, by the sign of these prosperous times, you have to visit to touch its balls. How does Fernandísimo not understand that, Antonieta and I ask ourselves! Wanting to go and die in New York! Absurd at that price and with a dollar that's increasingly difficult to obtain due to all those Chinese who are spreading all over the world with their efficient cheap labor! But that's not all. The most serious thing is that what one of those Marilyn-type blonde dolls there in Gringoland entraps him and entrances him until he decides to leave her his entire fortune?

All of these subtleties flew around my mind as Antonieta and I ran naked through the trees, anxious to see whether or not our car had been stolen. We had left it parked well beyond the edge of the half-hidden lake in a clearing surrounded by a fairly dense grove of trees. The worst thing was that we couldn't exactly remember the location. We couldn't see the wood for the trees or the trees for the wood. We came to one place and there was nothing. Was it the wrong place or had the car been taken? Oh, my God, it was actually over there. No, Antonieta, over that way. And we went in both directions and found nothing again. Not a sniff of the car, which was yet to be paid off in many installments that were anything but cheap. Antonieta was about to burst into tears and I was already screaming obscenities. Finally we discovered that our thieves were considerate and well-mannered people. We eventually realized that at last we had arrived at the right place when we saw that the car was gone but, nailed to the trunk of a pine, was an enormous sheet of paper written in German Gothic letters that read: Thanks for the car. You'll have to work hard to buy another one, but don't forget that ARBEIT MACHT FREI. And below they had the courtesy to put in brackets "WORK WILL SET YOU FREE".

Antonieta screamed hysterically and in the loneliness of that place it seemed like the breathless language of a hyena, so much so that her tits rose up and down and vibrated from right to left and her teeth chattered: "...And what are we going to do now?" I took a little time to answer her.

— Well, we'll go naked to the road, hitch a lift and see if they take us to the Plaza de los Reyes mansion, which is the closest place to here.

Antonieta hesitated, wiped her tears and looked around.

— We can't be naked on the side of the road, or even get to Fernandísimo's place. Aren't there any vine leaves around here?

— No, this isn't exactly the Garden of Eden, and you and I aren't Adam and Eve either.

Antonieta exploded, just like so many other times when the subject of Chile came to mind.

— I think I already realize this isn't the Garden of Eden! This is the shitty country where we live and of course we aren't Adam and Eve, but two poor and sad Chilean victims of the trash into which they've turned this country, those sons of bitches of politicians, the corrupt caste of the left and right, thieves and shameless criminals! We're two poor fools, naked, dispossessed by thieves who have every advantage because they're protected by idiotic laws that favor them... Two poor fools living in a shitty country.

— I'd say something different, sweetheart. Chile is a great country that's in the hands of shitty people.

The nearby noise of vehicles on the highway passing at great speed reminded us that it was better to get there and see about solving the problem before it got dark.

— Alright —mumbled my wife—, let's get to the highway. We've got no choice but to face the embarrassment... with dignity, though! Let's get going.

I stood there with flaccid arms hanging by my sides and lowered my eyes to look at the tips of my feet.

— Wait, Antonieta. Not yet. I can't just now.

— What's wrong with you?

— Haven't you noticed? Give me time for my erection to go away. I think I might have the beginnings of priapism.

Chapter 5

I can confirm with ABSOLUTE certainty. Fernandísimo Plaza de los Reyes was a dreamer and credulous of even the impossible. Despite his advanced age –seventy-two– he not only believed in elves, mediums, fortunes told with crystal balls, paranormal powers, and forces of good and evil present and hidden in the invisible, but he also continued to believe in whatever he believed despite obvious, objective, irrefutable and concrete proof that demonstrated that what he believed was nothing more than a lie or a treacherous and skillfully mounted falsehood. And so it was with Madame Chantal.

Around sixty years of age, Madame Chantal had become famous on national television. She had been the face of The Psychic of Paris on one of the most important TV channels. All of Chile watched the program, with a 97 percent rating of audience, who swallowed the fraud, sponsored, patronized and broadcast by the state channel and with the respected consent of the National Television Council, which was responsible for ensuring that Chilean television was a means of educating the public.

Madame Chantal was a Frenchwoman who had resided in Chile since the socialist Salvador Allende was elected as President of the Republic by a minority that didn't even reach 50 percent plus one of the suffrage, who, after three years of his term, was deposed by a military coup, the justification for which was that Allende had gone beyond the boundaries of the constitution to govern and, among other things, because military intelligence had discovered that weapons and 14,000 guerrillas had been brought in from Cuba in order to carry out an internal coup and thus implement a Marxist system in Chile by means of force. The Chilean armed forces, claiming their doctrine was republican and democratic, and adducing that the imposition of Marxism in the nation was an attack

13

on its sovereignty and internal security, proceeded to launch a coup on September 11 of 1973, culminating in the expected success and General Augusto Pinochet Ugarte coming to power as the head of a military junta. And, lastly, the most important justification for what was called the Military Pronouncement (or in other words, the Coup!) was that a significant majority of Chileans were crying out for the intervention of the military to overthrow the disastrous government and because they openly refused to live in Chile as a satellite of Cuba under the Marxist system. In addition, not only did the people on the streets cry out for this by banging pots and pans and calling the generals "chickens" for their initial impassivity, throwing corn into their front gardens, but the Christian Democrat Party, the overwhelming majority in congress did so too. The funny thing about this is that it was the support of that same party that allowed Allende to govern with the minority of votes he had obtained. Well, the loyalties of Chilean politicians to their people! Fernandísimo Plaza de los Reyes incidentally remembered all these details and they accentuated the pain of his duodenal ulcer, urging him even more strongly to go to New York and die there. And to top it all off –he shouted to Mr. Bob– the same people came back and now they govern under a democracy to steal money from Chileans, giving free rein to corruption, rolling out the red carpet for criminals, for the use of the privileged class to transgress equality before the law and underhandedly try to re-impose their shitty system! No, Bob, I'm going to die in New York. I don't want my corpse to rot with all the garbage that pollutes the soil of this country because this country was contaminated by a rabble of corrupt and shameless scoundrels!

The Frenchwoman Simone Chantal, a leftist militant in her home country, had come to Chile to see and hopefully participate in the only socialist revolution in the world that had come to power by a democratic vote, although, as I said, its election was not achieved by absolute majority, but rather a relative one. An experiment with Marxist-style socialism achieved by a democratic vote? That caught the attention of the world and, of course, the attractive and graceful little Frenchwoman Simone Chantal. The Allende government was marked by demonstrations both for and against its mandate, due to shortages that government supporters attributed to a boycott by right-wing businessmen, farmers and manufacturers, and which the right attributed to government ineptitude and social turmoil, disorder

and internal insecurity. Simone, who was later to become The Psychic of
Paris, took advantage of the troubled times to free herself of all restraint
and have indiscriminate sex with both Moors and Christians, communists
and nationalists, moderates and esteemed members of the ultra-left, with
artists of Chilean new song[1] with social and political content, and even
with Creole singers of blues and rock and roll. She swayed her ass to the
rhythm of the songs of Silvio Rodríguez and Victor Jara, as well as the
beat of Danny Chilean, Marcelo and even to the sound of Los Huasos
Quincheros[2]. It could be said that in those days of youth and lasciviousness,
she applied herself to achieving transversal sexuality, with no prejudices
or political distinctions, without discriminating between civilians and
military, between right-wing collaborators, fascists and feverish leftists.
She subjugated the three fascisms: the right, the left and the nationalist.
Her sexual surrender had been generous, freethinking and conciliatory, so
to speak, enjoying men simply because they were men without concerning
herself with their fanaticism, their ravings, their utopian dreams, or their
pretentions of grandeur, fame, power and wealth, or their selfishness and
vested interests. Thanks to having so many different men between her legs,
she learned that all men are the same during moments of intimacy and the
rest is just a mask to entertain oneself with a little adrenaline in the blood
with the dangerous and hectic game of life.

— The only nonsense I can accept from you, gorgeous, is your desire
for me —she would say in that French accent to her various lovers as a
necessary ritual prior to getting naked on the mattress, culminating with
her tongue licking slowly and greedily across her lips. Then came the
debacle, and sometimes, depending on the number of participants, Sodom
and Gomorrah.

But the years don't go by without taking their effect and her elegant
and discreet prostitution wilted along with her body and she eventually fell
into poverty. In a neoliberal society with a thriving free market economy,
everything is fine until you stop earning a good salary and as social support

---

[1] A social movement and musical genre in Latin America characterized by folk-
inspired style and socially committed lyrics.
[2] A popular Chilean folk musical group considered to be standard-bearers for the
most conservative right-wing sectors of Chile and thought to represent the military
regime.

in Chile appears to be nothing more than a pleasant slogan, the Madame began almost literally starving to death. After she had spent the last peso of what little she had saved, given the frivolity with which he had lived, she spent his first homeless night in the street; more accurately under a bridge over the river Mapocho. Of course, it wasn't one of the bridges over the Seine in Paris, which would have offered her a better class of homelessness, but what was she going to do? She was in Santiago de Chile and that was all there was, as the Chileans often say in their historical and chronic spirit of resignation. That night, huddled against the cold wall of ancient stones under the bridge and with the gurgling of the murky river water for ambience, she fell asleep as she sang to herself in what was a barely audible whisper; La Vie en Rose.

Simone Chantal, at that moment a vagrant and later The Psychic of Paris, opened her eyes very early at dawn and the first thing she saw was the tall sky-blue turban. The sound of the river suddenly sounded loud in her ears, which brought her to a fully wakened state. It was then that she saw the thick, graying beard and the tall, thin, dark-skinned man with the light-blue turban standing beside her staring.

— Tarud Arab.

The sound of the river had grown louder so she made a deaf gesture with her hand and ear.

— Tarud Arab.

— Pardon... what?

— My name is Tarud Arab. A pleasure. You will no longer have to sleep in the street. I will take you to my house.

The river splashed loudly again.

— Pardon... I won't have to what?

The man in the turban almost shouted:

— You won't have to sleep in the street. I'll take you to my house.

— Why?

— Because I am Tarud Arab, the magician, the psychic and I have felt that you have extrasensory powers.

— That I have powers... what?

— You are a psychic and you don't know it. Come with me.

Tarud Arab took her hand and lifted her, almost jumping, to her feet, and without letting her go, led her towards the ladder up the wall.

— My name is Simone Chantal.

— I know. I knew it when I saw you a little while ago up on the bridge. Go up.

And up they went. At that moment, one could say, the first link was created in the chain that would unleash the great madness in the mind of Fernandísimo Plaza de los Reyes.

Chapter 6

The police are kinder than any other type of citizen in this country, but they never showed up, thank God, for reasons I'll mention later. Antonieta hid behind a bush beside the road while I stood impudently naked at the very edge of the road, thumb out so someone would stop and agree to give us a ride. But the vehicles sped past and from the windows they pointed at us with their fingers, laughing their heads off and shouting all sorts of nonsense and insults. "Shit, you've got a small one, dude, it looks like clitoris. Hey, the chick behind the bush, are you pissing or shitting? If you want, asshole, I'll give you a ride, impaled on this pole. If you let me fuck the chick, we'll take you, shithead." I felt humiliated, indignant, overpowered by the impotence of not being able to defend myself, of not having the possibility of kicking in the heads of these human scumbags until they split. With every insult, with every obscenity that came from the snouts of those badly raised animals, I was more convinced that Fernandísimo Plaza de los Reyes had every reason to want to leave and die in New York rather than in this shitty country. During those hellish moments I had to suffer I thought about what little use it was to Chile to have such diverse and incredibly beautiful nature if most of its people were so ignorant, coarse and rude. I remembered how that scum, now with free market purchasing power and the credit of plastic money, had gone abroad to Argentina, Peru and other countries, and how many had been detained by the Peruvian or Argentine police for having scribbled vulgarities or obscene pictures on solemn and significant monuments. Lovely ambassadors of Chile! They were the people we were producing while the lying and corrupt political class filled their pockets and mouths talking about the quality of education and social justice for the people. Blah blah blah blah. Just before the two men who wanted to rape us stopped their pickup, I remembered the thoughts of an American philosopher, W.R. Emerson, who maintained that the quality of a country was measured not by its material achievements but by the kind of people that country produced. Ha! Chile's current score wasn't the best, for sure! It was a white pickup truck that began to slow down quite a long from where I was. The person behind the wheel had surely noticed my total nudity long beforehand. I covered my now flaccid and drooping private parts with both hands and prayed that whoever was driving wasn't a woman; old or young it didn't matter, but she mustn't be a woman. In such situations all the embarrassments in the world are reduced to one. The truck moved increasingly slowly until it stopped, almost touching me with the fender. I sighed in relief. Through the windshield I saw two men. The driver was a substantial man with a thick, graying beard, bulky in every way; head, neck, shoulders, arms, abdomen, hands, and certainly even his aura. A ton of muscles, fat and bones and spirit, if the spirit weighs anything. Although difficult to be exact, I guessed he was in his fifties. His companion was a very dark young man, with intensely black, thick hair. He had, as they say, nail-like spikes; he looked like a hedgehog. As I saw them both laughing at me, I could see that hedgehog boy had two conspicuously missing front teeth in the upper row. The ton of meat, bones, fat and hair spoke to me without ceasing his laughter.

— What happened to you, buddy, for fuck's sake? Did the stork just drop you or did they catch it flying low and shoot it down?

It took me a few seconds to answer. I looked at the bush and couldn't see Antonieta. Had she fled into the woods?

— We were robbed.

The big man frowned.

— We...? So there's more than one of you?

— There are two of us.

— Two? Your brother, your son, a friend? Where's the other one?

— Behind that bush.

— And why doesn't he show himself? What a timid guy!

The young man with the hedgehog hair interrupted. His voice was sharp, shrill, strident, and his speech instantly carried an unpleasantly mocking tone.

— Maybe the other one's a total faggot... hahaha... and it wouldn't be strange if this one was too.

— Shut up, idiot, be serious. We have to help these friends.

The word friends and the change of attitude of the large man made me feel a little more confident and, anxious to be inside the pickup as soon as possible and stop exposing my nudity on the public highway, I informed him.

— The other person is my wife.

Like a flash, a suspicious and peculiar glint suddenly flashed in the eyes of the bearded man. The other guy gave him a subtle glance of complicity. The big fellow couldn't conceal his enthusiasm.

— Ah, your wife! That's very good! Tell her to come out and get in. I'll get you out of this mess and take you where you can get some clothes. You're among friends who are happy to help. Right, Santurrón?

Santurrón replied with a mischievous wink and the large man responded with a laugh that he intended to demonstrate satisfaction and friendship, but which seemed more like something else to me. At that moment I realized that I'd made a terrible mistake.

Chapter 7

Madame Chantal, The Psychic of Paris, looked like a witch from some Shakespearean play. An old woman, face creased with wrinkles and a hooked nose that, curiously, she seemed not to have had when young. Her very blond and rather thin and untidy hair hung from her head and she leaned in an attitude of ecstasy over the crystal ball placed on the elegant and highly expensive coffee table. In the middle of the semi-darkened room, stood a huge and luxurious bookcase-desk, with high shelves of carved mahogany filled with tomes bound in fine leather, just a few steps behind Fernandísimo Plaza de los Reyes, erect in his fine, slender form, with the usual classic elegance. He had reached seventy-two years with solemn dignity, bearing, poise and charm.

The Psychic of Paris suddenly raised a hand beckoning him to come close and gesturing towards the crystal ball.

— Come, Don Fernandísimo. Hurry, there is something here for you. Sit there, in front of me.

Fernandísimo Plaza de los Reyes sat staring at the ball.

— I don't see anything. I just see you, all deformed through the glass. Because that thing I can see is you, I suppose.

— If it's a thing, then I suppose it is not me. What is in there is your face.

— My face? I thought it was yours.

— You cannot see anything that gravitates within the sphere. I am the one who sees.

— Yes right. You are the seer, Madame. What's going on? What's there?

The Shakespearean witch remained silent for a moment. Suddenly she uttered an exclamation and lifted both hands to her startled mouth.

— I no longer see your face! ...Oh, dear God!

— What do you see! ...What happened to me? What's there?

— A war is coming.

Plaza de los Reyes sighed with relief. That's all it was, a war. Just as well, nothing special, quite the opposite. Peace returned to his spirit.

— A war. Against whom? Against the Bolivians, against the Peruvians or against both, in addition to the Argentines? He smiled as he asked.

— It is a terrible war.

— Madame, every war is terrible. But it's always others who fight them. Never oneself. And certainly not those who declare them.

— But this is an even more terrible war.

— Please, Madame, finish for once and for all! You like suspense! Who is this war against?

— Against North Vietnam.

Although he would never have allowed it previously, the thunderous laughter into which Fernandísimo Plaza de los Reyes broke with unusual spontaneity literally caused Madame Chantal to jump from her seat. She must have confused that explosion with a bombing during that terrible war against Vietnam waged within the magical interior of the crystal ball.

— Hahaha... But how would Chile be at war with Vietnam? That's thousands of miles from here! Besides, it's a single Vietnam because as you have...

At that point, Plaza de los Reyes suddenly interrupted his speech. He had just realized. His change of mood was abrupt. And out it came like a blast:

— Madame, you're lying to me! There is no North Vietnam now. If you want to lie, inform yourself of the history first.

— Do not insult me. Here, what is happening is the war the United States of America is waging against the Vietcong in support of South Vietnam.

Fernandísimo Plaza de los Reyes stood up in a gesture of even more fury. This was the height of shamelessness and deceit. He rushed to the exit door of the library and flung it open.

— Get out. You're a liar, a swindler, a walking fraud. What do you think I am, stupid?! How can you say you see the future in that ball! The Vietnam War ended more than forty years ago! Forty years, Madame, forty years!

— I know and I am not ignorant. I was born and raised in Europe, sir, if you had forgotten —she said, emphasizing her French accent even more.

— Ah...! You're not ignorant! Born and raised in Europe! Born and raised under the bridges of the Seine surely...! Ah! And... do you want to tell me what I have to do with that war?! Nothing, Madame, nothing! When it happened, so you know, I hardly knew about it because of the lousy and biased journalism in this country that's not "sub-developed" but "infra-developed"! Yes, sir, infra... infra-developed!

Simone Chantal did not reply. In spite of her witch-like features she adopted an air of monarchic dignity. In a silence worthy of a cathedral and in which only the sharp panting of Fernandísimo Plaza de los Reyes could be heard, she opened her bag, picked up the crystal ball as if she had just discovered the Holy Grail and placed it inside with great solemnity. She stood up and with a gait like a bishop praising the pope, her back straight, straw hat on her head, she crossed the threshold of the door. At that instant, Fernandísimo Plaza de los Reyes remembered who he was.

— Madame... Madame... You must understand, Madame, that at my age I can't accept that I should be deceived with impunity. Understand me... I watched you on all of your TV shows, I admired you, I had faith in your psychic and predictive powers, I called you to provide me with your services, I offer you a not inconsiderable sum, practically sixty times more than you charge... and look... you coarsely trick me... Madame, I'm not an ignoramus. The Vietnam War...! Anyway, excuse the outburst... It's not my style to shout or offend...

She stopped without turning toward him. There was a brief silence.

— Go in peace... Good-bye, Madame.

She took her time and turned to him and Fernandísimo Plaza de los Reyes faced her once again. The Psychic of Paris. Her eyes penetrated him with a look from the dark depths of infinity and the very origins of the universe. The man gulped and was left speechless, static, almost hypnotized you could say. He waited.

— You have committed a grave mistake —began the Psychic sententiously, with an intentional heavy French accent. The Vietnam War is not yet over for the United States of America, and you, incredulous monsieur, will have much to do with it. And not only in this, but in many other events of recent years that are historical milestones that are more than important to that country in which you are so interested.

— Madame, I don't know what you're talking about, but try to understand me...

— I repeat, you have made a grave error. In life, monsieur, one must not be rushed. I am surprised that you should be so at your age and with the education you seem to have.

— It's because I've been a bit nervous... My dog, Mr. Bob, has been sick and neither Antonieta nor her husband Ricardo, my only true friends, have come to visit me... and this has been going on for days... and well... I also had a horrible nightmare about them. I dreamed that they were robbed and left completely naked on top of a mountain peak in the Andes.

— The apologies aggravate the mistake, monsieur. It's too late. You have lost it. Valuable information for you came to me which would have helped you to fulfill your fondest dream: to live and die in New York completely legally. You heard me correctly, didn't you? Completely legally. But you lost it. You have offended me. And do you realize who you have offended? Someone with psychic powers!

Fernandísimo held his breath when he heard that last sentence. He hadn't considered the consequences of yelling at the person he had yelled at.

— And not only that —she continued after a second of suspense. Do you realize that you have offended a television celebrity? Do you consider that? You have offended none other than The Psychic of Paris, I, Simone Chantal, who has the highest ratings on Chilean television, who is more popular and trustworthy than the President of the Republic herself! Measure your words and impulses next time, Mr. Plaza de los Reyes and honor your ostentatious surname! Goodbye.

Once again she turned her back on him and began walking away with a determined and rapid step. She was about to reach the exit of the immense mansion when she stopped on hearing the desperate wail that came from behind her, emanating from the trembling mouth of Plaza de los Reyes, who had followed her through the broad and long entrance hall, almost slipping on the glittering marble floor.

— Waaaait... Waaaait...

And once he was within reach of her.

— Wait, please... I beg you... I ask a thousand pardons... Madame, please, whatever you want, let's continue.

— For how much more money, monsieur? Now the price is different. Offenses deserve redress.

If it was money, he had more than enough. But at the same time one had to take care of money. It isn't a matter of splashing it around as like someone who takes off his hat and throws it onto the ground. But the most precious dreams cannot be left aside for a matter of money. Or can they? On the other hand, there's no need to neglect the security of existence. That woman had let slip a subtle threat. Do you realize who you have offended? She had said that before concluding with a very particular and disturbing tone... someone with psychic powers!

— How much more, Madame?

— Hmm... I do not want to take advantage of you. It could ten times more than you had already offered me. But I am considerate. Let's leave it at seven times more. It is an esoteric number.

Plaza de los Reyes moved his eyes from one side to the other and finally, fixing his gaze on any point that wasn't her face, he began to ask a series of questions.

— So you're not lying to me?

— I am no gypsy, sir.

— And you claim to me that the United States has not yet ended the war with Vietnam. That sounds strange, don't you think?

— It does sound strange, yes, but you will soon understand why. It is most interesting and especially for you.

— And you assure me that I am involved in all this?

— Yes, dear sir, it is so. You have a great deal to do with the current war that the United States still wages in Vietnam.

— But that war hasn't been mentioned on CNN.

— There are many things that are ignored or not mentioned on CNN. In this case, CNN is ignoring the issue. It is impossible for me to know.

— But you know.

— Sorry, I am much more than CNN and any journalist. I am psychic, I am The Psychic of...

— ...Paris, yes I know.

— So?

— So what?

— Are you a little slow, or are you pretending, monsieur? Do you agree to continue the session for a sum seven times higher than we had agreed?

— One last question.

— Go ahead.

— And as I have something to do with all this underground war or whatever it's called, will I end up having legal papers to live and die in New York?

— Monsieur, not just legal residence, but American citizenship!

— I accept!

Chapter 8

It was a pickup with a double cabin, so Antonieta and I sat in the back. We were still naked. The two men hadn't even been kind enough to throw us so much as a blanket, and when we asked for one, the big guy behind the wheel said, laughing, "What do you want to cover yourselves up for? You'll be cooler as you are." And Santurrón chimed in with his laughter. We suddenly noticed that the pickup had left the paved highway and was heading inland on quite a narrow dirt road that led steeply up towards a tall mountain. Antonieta squeezed my hand and whispered very quietly.

— Ricardo... where's he going? I don't like this at all... I've got a bad feeling. Last night I dreamed that Fernandísimo was dreaming that we were stripped naked on a mountain, that someone robbed and raped us.

— They raped us...? Me too?

— Both of us. Diversity isn't looked down upon these days. And then I saw Fernandísimo flying over that mountain in a Superman suit and he rescued us by taking down the two gorillas who'd raped us...

— Gorillas!

— ...he put us on his back and flew back up toward the clouds, but not before planting a United States flag on the summit.

— Well, but it was really just a dream.

— But this pickup is getting further and further away from civilization and it's going up this mountain and as far as I know we're not dreaming, Ricardo.

— No, I suppose not. I wish it were just a nightmare and we'd wake up sleeping in one of Clark Kent's.... I mean Fernandísimo's rooms.

The truck jolted along its now tortuous ascent and the silence into which both men had fallen began to instill me with panic. All we could hear was the roar of the engine and the two huge wrenches that were in front of us the back pocket of the driver's seat. The clanking of metal was driving me crazy, but apparently not Antonieta, who had been staring at them as if in a trance. I thought I understood. She has always been a fan of metallic sounds. She always loved the noise of an electric grinder when sharpening a knife, or the sound of steel when two swords clashed against each other in full battle in Stewart Granger's movies as Scaramouche or the Dalai Lama-like vibration of some oriental metal bowl. And I wasn't mistaken. She whispered in my ear "at least the noise of those two tools is lifting my spirits" and then she shot me a smile despite the desperate situation we were in. I was unable to answer because just at that moment the truck gave such a violent lurch that I sprang out of my seat, cracking my head against the roof. "Ow!" And Santurrón turned to look at me just as I was rubbing my head with a face of suffering. He giggled in a way that seemed quite effeminate to me, worrying me greatly, and then he said something to his bearded companion gripping the steering wheel, who spat out a laugh that made me imagine all his teeth and molars crashing against the windshield and smashing it to pieces. But no, the glass remained intact and, with absolute certainty I would say, his mouth remained full of teeth.

As we climbed, the road became narrower, steeper and stonier. On the right side, opposite the driver's door, there was a sheer wall of mountainous rock and on the left side the precipice was almost endless and not without a feeling of vertigo. Looking out of the window I had the impression of flying in a small, fragile plane at high altitude. I could say here that I was gulping, as a full-blooded narrator would have written, but since I'm just an amateur attempting to give an account of the life of Fernandísimo Plaza de los Reyes, I'll say that I had a knot in my stomach. I hadn't finished getting over that fright when I had another that was even worse. The pickup stopped. The big man switched off the engine and let himself drop out onto the ground like a sack. Santurrón did the same with an agile jump, rather too effeminately for my liking, scaring me once again. They had stopped right in front of a kind of cave, the mouth of which opened into the rock of the Andes. Antonieta and I looked at each other and she winked. I didn't have any idea what she meant by that wink. I doubted that she was flirting with me. But then maybe she was as a way of giving me a last loving wink before dying, raped by those scumbags. So I winked back, but as a funereal, tragic, posthumous gesture. I acknowledge that it's difficult to wink in that mood, but I know I managed it because of the face

30

of immense exclamatory and interrogative signals with which she replied to my romantic farewell.

Without a word, the two degenerates opened each of the rear doors of the pickup. Antonieta was faced by the big man and for me, it was what I had feared, Santurrón, the homosexual. With horror we saw that they both had their penises out and were threateningly erect. As if a protocol of professional criminals, the one-ton bearded man announced almost solemnly: "This is a rape." "Thank you for the courtesy of announcing it with due anticipation," I managed to say before hearing the imperative, almost military cry from Antonieta: "The wrench!" it was only then that I realized how slow I usually am and finally I understood everything. Now I appreciated the reason why Antonieta had seemed so self-absorbed as she stared at the tools as they clanked together, her comment about how the noises had raised her spirits, and why she had winked at me. Of course she wasn't flirting. It was a communications signal in full operation, worthy of United States Navy SEALs. I shuddered at the thought that she was much smarter than me and that, at the moment when we murdered each other because of the inheritance we expected, she was going to be one step ahead of me and the only thing I would receive from that fortune would be a lavish and luxurious funeral. But I reacted just in time and, in sync with her, I took the wrench and before Santurrón had time to grab my genitals –let's not forget that I was naked– I struck him a ferocious blow on the head. The young man didn't even cry out because his head split open like a watermelon and he fell to the ground scattering what little intelligence he must have had onto the ground. Treading on his meager ideas and clichéd thoughts strewn across the ground, I turned to see what was happening with Antonieta. The first thing I saw was that I couldn't see her. But I did hear her screams and the grunts of the big man. I climbed onto the hood of the pickup and there they were, struggling together, rolling over the rock toward the edge of the cliff. My Machiavellian thought was that if both of them fell off the cliff, Divine Providence would have spared me the task of committing murder against my wife when the long-awaited time came for Fernandísimo Plaza de los Reyes to die. I looked up to make sure that our millionaire friend wasn't about to come flying down dressed as Superman to ruin Divine Providence's work. It was going exceedingly well. No one came flying out of God's skies, so I simply continued watching the battle

31

between my wife and her rapist, lying comfortably on my stomach across the hood, waiting for them both to tumble into the void. The alibi was perfect. "The men kidnapped us, they took us into the mountains, we fought against them, and suddenly everything went black. When I woke up, Your Honor, I saw the boy with his head smashed in a few yards away. I looked for my wife, I ran to the cliff edge and there, at the bottom, I realized that there were the two dead bodies of my beloved Antonieta and that bearded animal, or even better, that lost sheep who had tried to rape us. May God receive them all in His Holy Kingdom. My poor, sweet and tender wife who had to become a vile criminal to try and save herself and mainly to save the life of such a worthless man as me, Your Honor. Maybe a sob would be good at that moment... "Do you realize, Your Honor? Do you realize what a weak human creature I am! Lacking the strength to save her and having suddenly fainted, leaving her alone with those two assailants! I deserve to be condemned for that, Your Honor! For life with no privileges, Your Honor!"

But suddenly, in one of those violent, whimsical twists of fate, the Devil or God, I don't know which, someone powerful mocked me. I heard a repetitious noise, sharp, shrill and desperate, like the squeal of a pig being castrated. I looked. It wasn't a pig, but something very similar. It was the thwarted rapist, as my wife was biting his genitals like a beast. I thought she was literally castrating him. It was no time to be jealous, but I did feel disappointed as I realized that the task of eliminating her when we received the inheritance was still pending and the truth is that I was already getting tired of thinking of how to do it in such a way that it would be the perfect crime. From what I saw next, she seemed to be just as unsubtle when committing murder as myself when I dispatched Santurrón. Taking advantage of the fact that the big man was writhing in pain, clutching his practically mashed genitals after being bitten by Antonieta, my future dead wife took the wrench and gave him a definitive blow to the head that not only left the unfortunate bearded man with his head literally cleaved in two, but literally dead, without any possibility of resurrection, even with the intervention of Jesus Christ.

— Bingo!

She looked at me and raised her thumb with the signal of a duty fulfilled.

— Bingo!

I thought that, if at the end of everything, after the non-voluntary departure of Fernandísimo Plaza de los Reyes, she was triumphant in our unshared or unspoken plans, she would repeat that gesture with one foot on my corpse and with a juicy wad of bills in her hand, brandishing them like a flag fluttering in the wind of victory after the war has been won.

— What do we do now?

She never hesitated. She always had a solution on the tip of her tongue:

— Burn these pigs with gas from the truck and burn the truck along with them.

— But without a truck, how will we get back?

— Walking. Don't you have two legs? And while we go down we'll talk. Come on, let's get to work!

And, not without difficulty, we lifted the bodies into the pickup, swept away the remnants of gray matter scattered on the ground and lit the fire, which was followed by an explosion and then an intense fire that surely left the robust guy without an ounce of fat.

Just after we just set out on the walk back, down the mountain, I said.

— This is my first crime.

— Mine too. For the first one it wasn't too bad.

Something sounded threatening in her comment, so I asked:

— Why did you say 'my first crime'? Are you planning to commit a second one?

No doubt she too felt threatened by my initial comment.

— And what did you say? Why did you say 'my first crime'? Have you got another one in mind too?

And so our conversation began as we went downhill.

— No, you answer me first.

— No, you first.

— No, you.

— No, you.

And so we continued.

— No, my dear, you first.

— No, honey, you first.

— No, you.

— No, you.

And by the time we were in the valley, near the road, it was coming to an end thus:

— You.

— You.

— You.

— You.

I had the slight impression that we not only suspected, but were also very frightened of each other.

Chapter 9

The hallway was very long and dark. It was an absurdly dark and absurdly long corridor. Nobody had ever thought to install a light bulb up on the high ceiling, but someone had thought to give it the length of a tunnel because whoever designed it apparently wanted to build a tunnel and not a corridor for a normal house. While Simone Chantal walked along it, preceded by Tarud Arab, she had the impression that she was entering a bunker. But that wasn't the case. The stupid tunnel ended just like any normal corridor at an aged spiral staircase that led to an old and wretched upper floor. There the daylight flooded into the interior through old divided-lite windows like a series of lockers, some rectangular, some square. Many of them lacked the respective glass, so cold air and rain poured through them in wintertime, and in summer the hot air turned the interior into an inferno, and in autumn and spring soft, warm, yellow leaves and lost butterflies fluttered in, as well as birds looking for a public to show off their songs, along with the fragrance of flowers and the rebirth of nature. Opposite those old windows, now impossible to open due to a lack of maintenance and cleaning, was a line of three adjacent windowless rooms with very high ceilings. At the back, and forming a sort of L-shape to the rooms, was the door that led to the bathroom (shower, black plastic curtain with fungus at the bottom, sink with cracked porcelain and a loose toilet bowl that had to be centered by hand before sitting on it) and next to the bathroom just a doorframe with no door that led into the kitchen. In there was a dishwasher whose only faucet dripped constantly and when opened gave way to a stream of water, causing a rumbling of pipes that were so ancient they seemed to be forcibly and painfully gargling. The rattling was so scandalously loud that it seemed the pipes were full of nuts and bolts rather than water. Next to this lamentable appliance, barely standing on its four rickety legs, was a table that had an unashamedly greasy surface and on that a modest gas cooker and a canister of the fuel could be seen. Hanging onto the peeling wall from their respective nails were a saucepan, a frying pan and a string of onions. A little further away, acting as a shelf, was a rustic table with two dinner plates, a soup bowl and a jug from which two teaspoons, a soup spoon, two knives and two forks poked out. Next to the jar was a cardboard box with detergent, and lastly, also hanging from a nail, a filthy kitchen cloth.

In the bedroom, there was a double bed and on the quilt, which must once have been white, Simone Chantal sat staring at the old wardrobe opposite to avoid the penetrating gaze of Tarud Arab standing before her. At that moment, Simone was considering that the point where the legs of that gangly man joined was too close to her mouth. It wasn't that she had any scruples, but first of all the guy didn't appeal to her and second, she didn't like to be deceived. These were things she thought of herself and that she believed very seriously. Things should be clear and dignity first. If he wanted to be a prostitute, then he should say so and if he wanted her to be a future psychic then he should tell her that too. But not both things together. Either prostitute or psychic.

— Oooh... aaah...

— Oooh... aaah... No, baby, not as a prostitute, no way, but as a clairvoyant naked in my bed, me between your legs just as I am now.

Tarud Arab had always been a man of action. First he acted and then he spoke. Or, like now, he acted while he spoke. She listened to him and answered with a tiny gasp between the grunts and groans and exaggerated cries of pleasure.

— Nice tits... I want you on TV as a clairvoyant.

— Ah, Ah, Ah... harder. On TV?

— I have good contacts. I will make you a star of fortunetelling.

— Aaah... Now you're making me see stars... come on, come on...

— You have to move fast.

— Yes, *mon cherie*, faster, because I'm about to come.

— No, not that. We have to move fast before somebody else beats us to it, somebody in television. There is a charlatan of a fortuneteller who walks around the TV station... Kiss me, kiss me, I want your tongue in my throat.

Then the dialogue was interrupted for a couple of minutes. There was only the creaking of the bed. And when her tongue was out of his mouth and back into her own:

— You will be Madame Chantal, The Psychic of Paris!

— Aah... oooh... aah... The Psychic of Paris? What will I have to do?

— Tell people's fortunes.

— Sweetheart, I don't know how to do it.

— You're doing it great, beautiful. Keep moving.

— No, not that. I don't know how to tell people's fortune.

— I will show you. It is a matter of imagination.

— Oooh... aaah... And what happens if what I tell them does not come true?

— It doesn't really matter. They will not notice. No one knows their future.

— But if what I tell them doesn't come true, then they will realize it is a lie.

— It makes no difference. By that time you will be far away with the money in your pocket.

— Ooohhh... aaahhh... Not so hard! But what if I can't get so far away?

— You will. You will guess their intimate future, their distant future that will take time to come true, but one day it will come.

— So you mean we will live a lie.

— Everybody lives a lie. The whole world is a lie.

— The whole world?

— Yes, my love, my love, my love... The only real thing is this... this... this... this... my love... now... now... I'm coming... aaaaah...

— Me too... My love, I'm coming, I'm coming... aaaaah...

— Deal...? Aaah.

— Aaah... aaah... deal, my love.

— Oh, aah... aaah... Aaaaaaaaaaaah.

— Aaaaaaaaaaaaaaaaaaaaaaaaah.

And the agreement was sealed. Thus it was that, Madame Chantal, The Psychic of Paris, was born to the world.

Chapter 10

Once again he was seated in front of her with the crystal ball in the center of the table. Everything was dimly light. Plaza de los Reyes was anxious. He was eager to know if his final destination would be New York and whether the earth of that beloved place would accommodate his corpse. A funeral in the most powerful country in the world isn't the same as one in an underdeveloped country. His cadaver deserved a top cemetery, with state-of-the-art technology and social and historical status. There were several of that nature in New York, but there was nothing wrong with being buried in Arlington Cemetery, even if it wasn't in New York. Even though Washington was Washington and it wasn't for nothing that he was none other than a Plaza de los Reyes, much better than those Errázuriz, Amunátegui, Larraín, Astaburuaga, Izaguirre and that whole bunch of rebranded Basques of whom there were so many in Chile, and the submissive, innocent and gullible Chileans, agreeing to put all of their laws, courts and systems to their service, revering and privileging them despite their vaunted equality before the law and their brand-new, trashy democracy.

After a long silence with her eyes fixed on the interior of the ball, The Psychic of Paris spoke, although in those instants her brain wasn't processing what her eyes were seeing, but what her heart felt: a huge, omnipresent dollar sign in all of her brain lobes.

— The first thing is a cancer —she said.

— A cancer?!

— Well, yes. A cancer. Don't you want to die in New York? Now we have the reason for your death. Fate is not chance, no coincidence is coincidence. It is a network of causes and effects that come together, ʼven from past lives. Actions you carried out centuries ago when you may have been a dragonfly or later a *moujik* on the Russian steppe, or perhaps an Egyptian pharaoh or a slave in the Roman arena or a Yankee hero in the Civil War, can be causes of effects and consequences in this, your present life. The cancer will make you a New York corpse and completely American, because, as I said, you will get more than a Green Card in the United States.

At that moment, Fernandísimo began to feel that the woman wasn't lying to him, that she really was a fortuneteller. Indeed, he had been diagnosed with cancer of the colon. He had consulted three serious, well-known and brand-name medical sources and all three had agreed on the same diagnosis. There was no doubt, Madame Chantal was honest. How could she have known about his cancer?

— What I can tell you, Mr. Plaza de los Reyes, is good news. Everything is heading toward the fulfillment of your wish: to die in New York. Luckily your cancer is already inoperable. It has progressed to metastasis, invading the testicles, so you will be needing little or nothing of them, and a tiny portion of the left lung, which is quite positive because that will induce you to stop smoking so that you cough less at night and particularly so you save money and stop supporting an evil industry based on vice, lies and excessive desire for profit. God bless you, Mr. Plaza de los Reyes!

As Madame Chantal said all this, she was internally grateful for how wonderful Google was, generously providing the information requested, and how useful those companies which, for a reasonable price, would sell you all the information you wanted about someone. That egotistical and bourgeois concept of privacy had long since been consigned to the past, thank heaven (or hell).

— Will I die honorably in New York?

— With all the dignity and pomp that a Plaza de los Reyes like yourself deserves. Remember, you will be a hero in the United States. You will become an important part of the history of that great country.

Fernandísimo lifted his eyes to the ceiling and smiled a beatific smile, seemingly mesmerized. He was brought back to reality by the voice of the fortuneteller.

— Why do you want to die in New York and not just go to live there?

He pondered the answer for a few moments.

— Because although you aren't given the choice of the place in which you want to be born, at least you have the possibility of choosing where you want to die. At least in most cases, unless you die a sudden death and in the least desirable of places.

— And, for you, Chile is the least desirable place?

— Yes, and not only to die but also to be born and to live.

— But this country is beautiful, monsieur. It has the loveliest landscapes, the best wines, which rival even those of France, my country, the most beautiful women, the mountains and the sea that calmly bathes it, in spite of the occasional tsunami.

— Yes, but it's full of Chileans. That's the problem.

From the room next to the library where they were sitting came three clear and sharp barks from Mr. Bob as support and corroboration in an act of absolute solidarity with the assertion of his master.

— And why do Chileans bother you so much, monsieur?

— Because of that, because they're Chileans. Being Chilean is a particular way of being almost different from the rest of the world.

— What do you mean, monsieur?

— To be Chilean is to be a mimicking monkey, you know? They feel proud not of what they are (because even they don't know what they are), but of feeling that they are like others, even if that's not really true. They say "we're the English of the Americas," but they're not punctual. They're a brown-skinned race, but the women, and even many of the men, want to be blond haired and blue-eyed, so those who work dying hair and selling contact lenses make a lot of money. They criticize the gringos and yet they construct enormous buildings, trying to imitate American architecture. The so-called upper neighborhoods are a pathetic imitation of Miami that's more Latin than gringo. Just imagine, they have even called a snobby area of the capital "Sanhattan", where they built a skyscraper to try and imitate the Twin Towers. If the gringos have their beautiful and traditional Manhattan, they don't want to be seen as being less with their Sanhattan. You realize: Santiago and from that the snobby Sanhattan. Pathetic. With people like that you can't live in peace.

— I see, monsieur. And you dislike Chileans purely because of that?

Hearing the question, Fernandísimo Plaza de los Reyes almost burst into flames. His cheeks reddened, the vein in his neck bulged, his eyes nearly popped out of their sockets, and the words erupted from his mouth.

— Tell me. Would you be happy with people who would rather say what's politically correct that say things how they are? Would you like to live with narrow-minded, provincial people who are astonished by anyone that's different to the majority? If you walk down the street with a top hat adorned with a beautiful colored feather on one side, a lovely red jacket, pointed shoes and jeans with ripped knees, all the idiots turn around to look at you, and there's no shortage of people who will ridicule you, saying something vulgar and rude like "did you run away from the circus, asshole? There's no respect, no tolerance or self-criticism. To be accepted you have to be man-sheep, be like the others, to be mediocre. Chileans are an ode to mediocrity, the champions of intolerance. Nowadays they give lip service to the slogan of respect for diversity, but that's all it is, just a slogan. Stupid government propaganda spread by the media that have all sold out to the interests of the dumb ruling class or the highest bidder. Just like all the corrupt politicians on the left and the right have sold out. In Chile today, profitability, money is worth more than people, you realize? And continue telling me, do you like to live among people who are envious of the talent or success of others? Begrudgery is an institution. If they see that someone is doing well, they pull them down. They lie or slander them. They do anything to make them fall from the position that they've managed to earn. There is no meritocracy, there's friendocracy, the so-called *pituto*[3]. You get a promotion because you're the son of someone or other, or because you're a friend of the minister or the manager of the company, or because you lent your ass to the faggot with power or to the womanizer who cuts the cake, in the case of a woman. You go up the ladder because you lobby and you suck the dick of the one who runs the show. That's why in this country second rate people are leaders and all the politicians are corrupt and contemptible; they're chosen by bunch of fools and idiots. You must have heard that people get the governments they deserve! Chile is a wonderful example of that, Madame. Would you like to be buried in the same soil as corpses who were mostly downright lousy in life? Not me! I have my pride and my dignity! Yes sir!

He literally spat this last sentence at her, as a few drops of spittle discourteously flecked the face of The Psychic of Paris.

---

[3] A Chilean term that refers to using one's connections to obtain something, usually a job.

— Monsieur, please, calm down because you're spraying me.

And with the dignity of an aging French woman, she dabbed at her cheek with a handkerchief and, while she was at it, the tip of her nose.

The crystal ball was still there at the center of the table, emanating its effusions of the future.

— I see something important here. Your leading role in the history of the United States of America.

— Good heavens!

— You are linked to the Vietnam War, the struggles in the Middle East, the Twin Towers.

— Me?

— You are a champion of the free world.

— With all due respect, Madame, I just hope that you're not taking me for a ride.

— If you make another one of those comments expressing doubt about my powers, I will suspend my services forever.

— Yes, sorry... okay.

— I was telling you that the Vietnam War is still going on for the United States. That is for two reasons. One is because there are veterans of that war. They need constant support: moral, psychological, economic. They are a reality that has to be faced. The other reason is monumental.

— Monumental!

— Yes. The Vietnam War was an expression of the crusade that the United States has always followed to defend freedom in the world against all forms of tyranny. It participated in the First World War, and then in the Second. Do you understand?

— Yes, I understand. But what do I have to do with all this?

She paused with great theatrical effect, leaned even further forward to see the innermost part of the crystal ball and then, standing up, stared straight into his eyes. The cuckoo of a German clock hanging on one of the walls made its call seven times in the half-dark. It was somehow the trumpeter heralding the crucial statement:

— You will be the one who finds the man most wanted by the Americans: Osama Bin Laden!

Chapter 11

Dante Carrasco Ugarte and his broom. The broom that he always carried on his right shoulder like a rifle was new and durable and he was a young man, thirty years old, tall, athletic, a military haircut, he looked energetic and had a pleasant and manly face. His affable smile with white, well-aligned teeth fascinated women and infected men with good humor. He was a loving and lovable person. However, he certainly wasn't one to mince his words.

Sometime people told him "you don't look Chilean, you have the look of those gringos from the movies that win the heart of a blonde beauty and beat up the bad guys." Dante was a little annoyed by these comments and usually responded with great energy and conviction. "Look buddy, I'm Chilean, more Chilean than empanadas, beans and red wine, and I'm not into blond chicks, but beautiful Chilean brunettes with waists and hips like a guitar that play our *cueca*[4] in the fields of our country." He was an epic individual, for sure. Many doubted his sanity. They couldn't understand why he always had a broom on his shoulder, all day and into the night. He had already earned the nickname "the loony with the broom". However, what struck people most about him was that when he was talking he was always coherent, sane, and correct in most of his opinions, although they weren't always in agreement with the feelings and thoughts of the majority. Unlike most Chileans, he didn't say what was politically correct, but what he considered to be true, necessary and fair. He was brave with his words, with his fists and, in a not too distant future, with his broom too, it was assumed.

---

[4] Traditional Chilean music, usually accompanied by a guitar, harp, piano, accordion nd tambourine.

— And, if you'll forgive the question, what's that broom for that you have on your shoulder all the time, buddy?"

— Well, to sweep up dirt, mister. What else did you think?

— The dirt in your house? Your house must be full of dirt then because I've noticed that the broom has been new for a while.

— No, not the dirt in my house. The dirt in Chile. Isn't Chile our home?

He had already become famous on the social networks. He had taken the time to upload photos of himself to Facebook with the broom on his shoulder and also with the broom at the ready like a Creole Don Quixote, prepared to right wrongs and protect widows and orphans. He also published his crusade for Chile on Twitter, writing things like "Chile isn't a shitty country, but a beautiful country in the hands of shitty people", "a good politician is a dead politician", "nowadays there are too many Chileans who are expensive goods and poor quality. They're sold to the highest bidder. The press has sold out, politicians have sold out, the armed forces and cops have sold out, the rats in management and the mice in middle management have sold out. Everyone sells out, except for Chileans willing to follow me with their own broom on their shoulder and be careful, there are plenty of us! He caused so much commotion on the internet that he finally managed to get the television people to seek him out for an interview.

— We'll give you five million pesos for the interview. How does that sound?

— I think that's wrong. I don't accept money for interviews. I'll be free to say what I want and I won't accept any editing cuts. It's the whole truth about what I think or nothing.

— But, Mr. Carrasco, the TV station thinks it's fair...

— Excuse me! Do you think that because I walk around everywhere with my broom that I'm an idiot? You're completely wrong. I know perfectly well that the objective of the interview is to neutralize the power of my message by making me look like a fool or a lunatic. You're part of the evil machinery interested in keeping good Chileans in ignorance to defend your petty economic interests and your anachronistic and decadent ideologies. You're the same as those who want Chile to remain the dump into which they've made it. Let me say all this and I won't even take a cup of coffee from you or there's no interview.

The people from the TV channel formed a circle like football players to come to an agreement before a game and in that ring of men talking head to head, they began to consider whether the sponsor of the program had been negligent in the terms of the contract and hadn't specified what the interviewee should or shouldn't say. They had solely specified the visual message of showing him with his ridiculous broom. They weren't going to miss out on a quite excellent payment from such a good sponsor and, as the man wouldn't accept the money, they would keep it for themselves. In the end, falsifying a signature for the reception of a fee wasn't exactly difficult. It was good business. And so the interview went on the air... live and direct!

Chapter 12

Since The Psychic of Paris had told him that he would be the key to finding the whereabouts of Osama Bin Laden, Fernandísimo Plaza de los Reyes decided that from that moment on his duty would be to remain glued to CNN – either the Spanish language or North American channel– to keep up to date on what was happening in the United States and particularly regarding the search for the wicked and cruel leader of Al Qaeda. He realized that there was little information on Osama Bin Laden. It wasn't much use for his purposes, to find clues that would help him end the search and thus be able to inform the American authorities. He became increasingly anxious, now not only to establish himself in the United States of America, but to become one of its heroes, to obtain American nationality and to die being afforded all the corresponding burial honors and, by preference, in Arlington Cemetery. This being the case, his colonic cancer could be considered a true blessing. But he had questions. The first: why was there so little information on television about the search for Bin Laden? The answer had been supplied by a retired military friend who had worked in the intelligence services during the dictatorship of General Pinochet. He had told him that the television channels would certainly have been ordered by the government not to broadcast information that might hinder the search operation and the intelligence work and that he would had to be careful with the information that did emerge because it would surely be disinformation intended to mislead. When his friend had asked why he was so interested in the subject and Fernandísimo told him what The Psychic of Paris had said, the former Chilean intelligence agent burst out laughing in his face. The millionaire and eager admirer of the United States of America felt offended and angry and told his friend to take a hike, telling him he was a "fascist soldier" and he pressed it home with "...I'm not afraid of you now and I can say exactly what I want to you because you don't have the sinister power you used to have." Still laughing, the ex-military man headed for the door and replied: "Since when did you become a communist? You ridiculous old man. You still believe in Santa Claus." On his way out he slammed the door hard. From outside, Plaza de los Reyes could still hear the guffaws of his former friend and even heard him apparently announce at the top of his voice to some passers-by: "The old man who lives there is even more moronic than a newborn dog!"

The second question was: If I do find the information, to which authority should I communicate it? Where do I start, with the police, the Chilean Foreign Ministry, the Consulate or the United States Embassy? Can you find the phone numbers of the Pentagon on Google?

However, the big, fundamental, and inescapable question was how and why he –Fernandísimo Plaza de los Reyes, who lived thousands of miles away from his great and beloved country– was going to obtain the key information to find the fugitive Osama Bin Laden? He didn't recall Madame Chantal having told him. It seems that she'd left something out and perhaps wasn't quite as professional as she claimed to be. He decided to call her on the phone to clarify the 'hows' and the 'whys' and that's when he realized that the Psychic was, undoubtedly, very professional.

— The information you require, Don Fernandísimo, has a new price. That would be an additional five million pesos.

Fernandísimo had to move the earpiece away from his head because the blow to his inner ear and brain had almost been a knockout. The famous Psychic had turned out to be a whore of divination!

— Five million more! Don't you think that's rather a lot, Madame?

— No, I don't think so. Think, monsieur, that this is information that we call privileged and it will open the doors to a splendid life for to you. Considering this, and you being a wealthy and respectable magnate of these latitudes, it is like giving a modest tip to a restaurant waitress.

— But Madame, you aren't exactly a restaurant waitress.

— Of course, monsieur. All the more reason then.

— Gulp!

There was a long silence. Fernandísimo wavered within.

— Monsieur Plaza de los Reyes, are you there? Did you have a heart attack?

— Guess if you are a real fortuneteller.

— No disrespect, please. Your money does not give you the right to do that.

— With all due respect, for what I'm seeing, these days my money gives me the right to everything or, vice versa, without money I have no right to anything.

— We shall come to that, monsieur. Progress is advancing at a rapid pace.

— Aha... one last question. Why did you retain the information I'm asking you for and why you didn't tell me during the session with the crystal ball that you had right in front you?

— Because if I had given you that information, you would not have called me, and I would not have had the opportunity to charge you another five million.

— At least you're honest.

— Every true fortuneteller must be honest, sincere and never lie.

Those words refortified Fernandísimo Plaza de los Reyes. Of course, the woman had her doctrine and her ethics.

— Very well. It's a deal. I'll pay you the five million. Now tell me what I asked: Why and how will I get the information about Bin Laden's whereabouts?

— You must come to my office with the five million in your pocket, in cash.

— Don't you trust me?

— No.

Fernandísimo breathed in a little more air than was usual and blew it back out like the snort of a tired bull.

— I'm on my way.

At the entrance of the house stood a large sign whose letters were apparently designed using a mixture of calligraphic styles: Arabesque, German Gothic and hints of biblical Hebrew characters. Despite the hodge-podge, there was a unity of design that immediately attracted the attention and could be read without difficulty: PSYCHIC AND SPIRITUAL ASSISTANCE. MADAME CHANTAL FROM PARIS AND ANCIENT ORIENT AND MIDDLE EAST. It was clear that the fortuneteller, concerned about her marketing, did not want to leave anything out and, being an exponent of Chilean snobbery, she wrote

51

everything in English. It was necessary to raise the level of the business in the eyes of national idiosyncrasy. Tarud Arab, her mentor, entrepreneur, exploiter and occasional lover had instructed her. You have to know how to sell, he had told her more than once. Everything can be sold, but you have to know how to do it properly. Nowadays even one's soul can be sold and not just to the devil, but to the highest bidder here on Earth.

The esoteric study of the Madame was fitted with lavish antique furniture of European origin and on the walls were large mirrors with white frames with arabesque forms. There were statues of angels, cherubs, mythological animals and, standing at the back, sculpted in what looked like glossy black marble, stood a majestic statue of Death, the skull covered with a cloak and the scythe gripped in the right hand. Such a thing would frighten anyone. Behind Death was a violet light, with a pink light emanating from behind, and at the back a white light shone out, seemingly being more than mere light itself. It appeared to be what we could imagine as a divine radiance. It was evident that such a lighting production had been designed by professionals. For a moment, Fernandísimo thought that perhaps the fortuneteller had hired special effects technicians directly from Hollywood. He could not conceive that something so nearly perfect, well done and rigorously complete could have come from anywhere other than the United States of America. His love for that great nation was blind and unconditional.

— Sit down, please, Mr. Plaza de los Reyes.

He sat across from her at the fine three-legged table. The crystal ball between them was four times larger than the one the Madame used for her home visits.

— Wow, Madame Chantal, this is a big one! Can you see more with it?

— Do not try to be funny, sir. This is a sacred and solemn place. There is no room for the profane here. Did you bring the five million?

Fernandísimo chose to focus his attention on the scent of sandalwood that gave fragrance to the ambience. That calmed him down and halted his urge to tell the Madame where to go. He opened the briefcase and put the succulent bundles of bills onto the three-legged table next to the crystal ball. The Psychic of Paris uttered a cry that one might imagine coming from a hysterical woman of the nineteenth century.

— Take that filth off there! You had better give it to me.

And, at startling speed, she took the stack of bills and left the room, saying to him from outside:

— I'm taking this profane treasure to the appropriate profane place.

Fernandísimo sighed in the silence and under the implacable gaze of Death there at the back looking at him. Would his colonic cancer lead him to face an image like that, at the last moment, emerging from the depths of the Hudson River some night as he crossed the lonely old Brooklyn Bridge? Well, at least it wouldn't be a mediocre death, but one worthy of a Plaza de los Reyes and his demise would certainly be published not only in the New York Times, but also in the Washington Post and, why not, in El Mercurio in Santiago de Chile too, as well as in the Valparaíso edition too, just so that nobody would be annoyed. Voices roused him from his ruminations. The first was the voice of a man outside with a slight Arabic accent:

— Did you count there was five million exactly?

The fortuneteller's voice replied immediately, pointing out that she had been in Chile for a long time.

— You think I'm stupid? There's five melons, right on the nose.

After that Madame Chantal came back in, with her strong French accent:

— Monsieur Plaza de los Reyes, excuse me. Let us restart our sacred session and let the profane continue with its turmoil, chaos and noise far from here, in the disorderly world of base desires, evil passions and limitless ambitions for fame, power and money.

This woman is certainly very versatile, thought Fernandísimo and he prepared to put all his faith in the lie so as to forget and not have to face life as the continuous present took place. To dream fabulous futures and magnify past memories that were not quite so fabulous is a practice in which most men waste their time, squandering the present and straining for what they would like to have or lamenting what they have failed to obtain in the past or for what was and no longer is.

— Hold my hands and look steadily into the ball.

He took her hands and stared into the ball. A melody with sounds from China began to be heard. The fortuneteller then uttered some words in a strange language. Perhaps the only language that was spoken before the Tower of Babel, thought Fernandísimo Plaza de los Reyes, whose imagination was stimulated by the theatrical ambience and, consequently, his credulity had increased exponentially.

— Zoímba lag tu, sharín camaché, Zoímba lag tu. Darna abba sharín me zim betzú, Zoimba lag tu. Utzá korbam abba sharín, abba sharinín der nosurto akahem, Zoímba lag tu. Zoímba lag tu, sharín camaché.

The speech ended in a very long soprano cry tinged at the beginning with hysterical tones that reached a climax of a very high frequency before declining softly and slowly in a kind of mournful melody. Charging another five million for the show undoubtedly merited a production comparable to a Broadway musical. The initial irruption of the unexpected scream caused Fernandísimo to leap from his chair and the subdued final sounds made him close his eyes as if her were a child listening to a lullaby.

— Dream…

— Oh Madame, I'm sorry, your song put me to sleep.

— No. I say the dream has come to me. It will be in a dream.

— What will be in a dream?

— The exact information on the whereabouts of Bin Laden will come to you through a dream. It will be a clear dream, more than real and you will remember it as soon as you open your eyes without forgetting it for an instant. With that information, you will be the future hero of the United States of America. As soon as you have it, the first thing you must do is tell the first New York police officer you see on the street. From then on, the links of the chain will come together on their own and the Americans will find the man they are looking for. The rest will only be glory for you.

The gleam that appeared in the eyes of Fernandísimo almost exceeded the brilliance of the divine light that the psychic had set up in her den of clairvoyance.

— Here I also see other mechanisms that could also be the ones that will lead you to find the information. It is the unconscious action of the pineal gland. In some way, the third eye.

— The pineal gland… the third eye?

— Well, it is a long explanation. But, in short, it means that you will have the information without knowing it, but at the same time, you will also be transmitting that information to others without knowing it. When the other receives the information, he will realize and will also know who sent it. If it happens by this means and not through a dream, the glory will still be for you.

Fernandísimo felt as if he had heard trumpets blaring triumphantly. A flash lasting millionths of a second came into his mind in which saw himself crowned with a laurel wreath, clad in a great white tunic embroidered with gold threads and seated majestically at the pinnacle of the Empire State Building. Down at his feet, New York with all that energetic potential of work and fun, of hope and despair, of success and failure, of dreams made real and dreams shattered against the indifference of the skyscrapers. Fernandísimo Plaza de los Reyes, emperor! The sidereal speed of human stupidity is incredible when expressing itself in the minds of men. And just as fast as it appears, so it is usually eternalized in the little heads of these creatures. No matter how much they have been taught and are taught, they never learn.

— And what about this third eye thing, shall I just do nothing? Will everything happen "without me moving from my desk"?

— Not quite, monsieur. Even if you do not have the information in your mind, you should make sure to look at a policeman from time to time, staring very hard for a few long seconds. It is very possible that at some of those times the information will be transmitted from your brain to the policeman immediately and he will realize. After that, the glory will be for you.

This time no trumpets sounded for Plaza de los Reyes, but a fundamental question came to him, the cornerstone of the whole matter.

— And tell me, Madame, how the hell am I going to know, by whatever means, about the whereabouts of this devilish fanatic I have never seen in my whole life except for the images on television? And why should it be specifically I who has that privilege, living thousands and thousands of miles from the United States and the Arab countries, whose names I barely know? Can you explain that to me?

She did not answer immediately. There was a long silence as she stared into his eyes. Fernandísimo feared that another explosion would come from her or he would receive kicks in the behind that would suddenly put him out on the street and he would have lost his five million. Distrust made a timid step back into his confused credulity. The Chinese sounds remained faint and comforting as the clairvoyant's calm voice emerged from her lips.

— There is what one calls destiny and predestination, monsieur Plaza de los Reyes.

— So…?

— Draw your own conclusions, monsieur. I cannot tell you more. You are an intelligent man.

Fernandísimo drew the conclusions that it suited him to draw. Of course, he was an intelligent man and what the fortuneteller told him was grand, glorious and splendid. There was no doubt, his conclusion was that the woman was right, that she was telling the truth and that as he was none other than a Plaza de los Reyes, he was predestined to something big, very grand here on Earth and, who knows, possibly later in Heaven.

When he was back on the street he felt that the bright light was blinding him. The sun was beating down hard right then. Lost in thought, he began to cross the road thinking about the glorious future that awaited him and remembering how to proceed when he was in New York. He repeated in an almost inaudible whisper: "As soon as you remember the dream, tell the first policeman you see on a street in New York"; "Look for policemen on duty and look them in the eyes for a few long seconds and await their reaction"; "As soon as you remember the dream…" He suddenly and unexpectedly jumped as he heard the violent braking of a car that had stopped a handbreadth from his face. The man at the wheel poked his big piggish head from the window and shouted: "Shut your piehole when you're crossing the street, you fucking old fool." Fernandísimo didn't delay in responding: "Shut your dirty mouth, you peasant. You're disrespecting a hero of the United States of America." The man with the pig's head retorted: "What have those fucking gringos got to do with me? This old man is even more stupid than a newborn dog!" And making his tires squeal, he sped off on his way. A few pedestrians who had stopped to enjoy the spectacle laughed at the "American hero." Fernandísimo looked at them defiantly and reproached them: "Very soon you'll know all about me… very soon!"

And as he continued down the street, he stopped in front of a window that caught his eye. There was a series of electronic devices, home appliances and televisions. On one of them, the one with the clearest image and a big screen, there was a handsome young man, with an athletic build and a brand new broom on his shoulder. He was being interviewed by a group of journalists and his gestures indicated that he was speaking with energy, strength and passion. What most astonished him was that behind the young man were a large number of boys, each holding Chilean flags that looked brand new, as clean as spring water and ready to flutter with joy. Without knowing why, he felt that the image was like an announcement of Chile's rebirth. Well, he said to himself, each to his own, which is why I'm going to New York. And off he went.

Chapter 13

Simone Chantal's early days on television as The Psychic of Paris had not been easy. After that first day of sex with Tarud Arab just after she had been rescued from under the bridge over the Mapocho, she had to endure many other days of a similar nature, each more twisted than the last and involving unspeakable sexual fantasies. The Kama Sutra became no more than a kindergarten manual and worst of all for Simone was that it all began to become repulsive to her. But she had learned a very true expression: "Necessity knows no bounds." However, she understood that it wasn't a simple need for subsistence. The man had promised her success, fame, money, luxury, splendor, and all of that, once promised, became a compulsive desire for her, an imperious and overwhelming need, a golden objective she had to achieve in any way she could. Despite her European culture, she never realized that someone called Machiavelli existed, but she did understand perfectly well that "the end justifies the means." As she had been a Marxist in her youth she fully agreed with that maxim and now, on the very threshold of prosperity and wealth, she had thrown away her stale Marxism as if discarding a pair of dirty, worn gloves at the dump. Now she was free to choose and, of all the options, she decided to walk the way of suffering before later enjoying. She had learned that with or without Marxism, or with or without capitalism, with any system that man invented, man is, has always been, and will always be a buyer and a seller. Cain and Abel wanted to buy God's favor somehow by offering him gifts. God chose to prefer to "buy" Abel's gift and, as a consequence, Cain grew angry and killed Abel. That was how the whole business of companies and competition had started, she thought. It wasn't much different now. The one who rises and is winning has to be stopped and hopefully eliminated from the competition. Man doesn't accept it when his brother does better than him. This, she continued thinking, was like that here and anywhere, now, before and tomorrow. And in this case her European culture had informed her who Rousseau was and consequently she knew that "man is wolf to man."

There was a time when she felt the wolf's presence right in her face. The wolf wore an Arabian turban and his name was Tarud Arab and he was sitting opposite her in a luxurious restaurant in the upscale area of Santiago. It was the evening, she had dressed up and he had invited her to dinner in order to hold the first interview with the television producer on whom he depended for approval of the planned program, "Know your destiny with Madame Chantal, The Psychic of Paris". The producer had looked over the project, listened to them, said he liked the program in principle, but hadn't promised them anything at the time. That was the moment in which he looked Simone Chantal up and down and admired her still finely shaped legs. During the interview, Tarud Arab looked at both of them, at the producer and at his promising fortuneteller, and he knew very well which steps had to be taken. Arab knew this business very well.

— Lobster, caviar?

— Lobster, caviar and champagne —she said with a certain mischief and some malice in her eyes and added— and French champagne, *s'il vous plaît*.

There was no reason why Tarud Arab's sexual indecencies and his desire for success and wealth at her expense should come cheaply. Like it or not, she would be the star of the show and she had to start to behaving as such. Besides, she'd never eaten lobster or caviar before.

The music was soft, the floor carpeted, a violinist played a romantic melody, the murmur of the diners at the other tables was restrained, prudent. It wasn't a place for stridency but a venue of refinement, and tapestries with equestrian motifs of a most British style adorned the walls. The soft and comfortable chairs were upholstered with silken fabric stamped with the same equestrian motifs as the tapestries. In the center of each table was a bronze lamp in the form of a horse's head whinnying to the sky and the light it cast was muted, discreet and intimate. It was an atmosphere for two and for two who were communicating very closely with one another.

— Tarud, what's the name of this restaurant?

— Equus, my little Frenchwoman.

Simone seemed to hear a neighing from some unseen speaker as part of the decoration and as if an advertising gimmick.

— What did you think of Di Giorgio?

— Di Giorgio?

— The guy we were talking to today. The producer of the television channel.

— Oh, yes... Well, fat and bald. Fake, I thought too.

— Well, Frenchie, you are going to start learning to like him. The guy is important. He is essential for our project.

While she frowned as her sole response, two waiters arrived with delicacies fit for an appetizer of kings. Another approached with a trolley to display the lobster so it could be approved by the gourmets and yet another presented the French champagne, showing them the label of the bottle with the same intention. Having received the gesture of approval from Tarud Arab, who bowed his head ceremoniously as a sign of confirmation, the waiters withdrew to return at the proper time with the promised feast.

— Why do I have to like that repulsive guy?

— Because, Frenchie, he decides who appears on the screen and who doesn't and besides, because of this...

He was silent for a few minutes and that made Simone anxious to hear the answer. In the meantime, he took off his moccasins, pushing them way with each foot and stretching his barefooted leg towards her legs. Rather than words from his mouth, in response Simone received his foot pressed practically into her vagina. The length of the fine tablecloth and the intimacy of the lighting concealed the outrage.

— Oh, but...!

— You get the message?

— I don't like your style.

— You will have to get used to it, Frenchie. In the world to which we are going, this is the style —and he moved his intrusive toe without decorum. There's just ratings, money and fame and, if not, a kick up the ass, poverty and oblivion.

— You're very philosophical. Get your dirty socks out of my panties!

Tarud complied.

— If what you wanted to say to me is that I have to sleep with that pot-bellied billiard ball, I'm afraid to disappoint you, but I won't do it!

— If you don't, the golden dream will become a soap bubble and then pop —replied Arab between clenched teeth and in a quick whisper, reinserting his big toe between her legs and this time not only without decorum, but with intentional and overt aggression.

— You're hurting me.

— Ha, pretentious bitch, you're talking they do in like the soap operas.

— Is this what you call a celebration dinner?

— Look, Frenchie, they're bringing the lobster now.

They were indeed bringing the lobster and the other delights with the champagne buried into the ice filling the silver bucket. It was the dinner for Little Red Riding Hood at the palace party of Cinderella whilst being courted by the wolf.

— Oh, but madam and sir haven't tasted a bite of the appetizer! Shall we take it away?

— No, put it under the table —said Simone.

Tarud quickly withdrew his foot from the warm place where it was nestled.

— Excuse me, what did you say, madam?

— Nothing. Never mind, it was just a joke. Leave it all here, please. We usually mix things together.

The waiters withdrew and the lobster sat there waiting to be eaten.

Tarud Arab poured some champagne into the fine carved crystal glasses.

— To us, my fortuneteller from Paris. From now on you and I are one and the one that we now are will inherit the kingdom of money, fame and splendor.

Simone drained her drink with a scandalous noise of liquid glugging down her throat.

— Say whatever you want, Arab, but I'm not going to sleep with the television guy.

— Not just with him, sweetheart. You will have to do it with several more. Three more at least. I know this business very well.

— You're a pig.

— You think so? Cheers!

As if that were the last supper, they began to share the lobster in a ritual of absolute silence. Something floated in the air while the violin was still playing its soft and mournful melody in the background. Something unspoken had been left between them. They felt that something was coming that would have to be expressed definitively, all or nothing. The beginning of an adventure towards golden horizons or the end of aspirations. For Tarud Arab, another unsuccessful business and for Simone, her return to freedom under the bridges of the Mapocho River. Tarud hurriedly sipped his champagne three times and filled her glass to the brim. In the silence the bubbling contents of the bottle could be heard swishing into the glasses and even the gurgling of the bubbles. She downed the contents in one. Arab glanced at her with genuine satisfaction and filled her glass again. She took no time to empty it once again. Arab again served her glass up to the top. And again she drank all the way to the bottom. Then the turbaned wolf asked for another bottle. The weapon requested was brought rapidly, with the bomb preserved in the chill of the crushed ice. Meanwhile, the lobster was gradually disappearing into their mouths and eager stomachs. Between swigs and bites, she was thinking over and over about the idea. Sleep with several men at once to become rich and famous? If only they were her type, but the specimen she had met was repulsive. The others could be even worse. Dignity? What's that about dignity? Isn't it just a word with prestige but doesn't actually mean anything? And if dignity existed and I didn't have it, would I die because of it? People die without bread or water, but without dignity? Well, I'm sure there's someone who'd say that. But does anyone live on what others say? Most of the people in this country of sheep, but they're still alive and kicking whatever they may say. Besides, people always say things, they come and they go. However, this is very serious and therefore it has to be taken into account: there is a God who is watching us. At this point in her reflections, Simone stopped with a piece of lobster in her mouth. The impact of this great assertion prevented her from swallowing. There were a few seconds of suspense and then an image jumped into her mind of herself dressed as a queen being hailed by a crowd of young witches with hooked noses, but all beautiful, blonde and blue-eyed and clothed in white silk robes. This finally allowed her to swallow the piece of lobster in her mouth and continue with her internal debate. Nevertheless, does God really watch us? Does He have time to do that? Is He so interested in us that He is willing to waste his time on it? And how can He look at each and every one at the same time if humanity is a crowd that escapes the capacity of every census? So is God an idle and indolent being? How can He see so much tragedy down here and do nothing to prevent it with all the power they say He has? And, ultimately, does God really exist? She heard Arab's voice saying cheers. She felt he was far away and saw him as distant and fuzzy. How many times had he said cheers? She felt it was time for the answer. The bridges of the Mapocho or the throne of the witches. Simone made an effort to fix her eyes on his and lifted her glass with a precarious balance that made her spill a little champagne onto the tablecloth.

— Joy, joy —said Tarud, hoping to hear some good news from her. Then Simone said to him:

— To us, my god and mentor, to you and I, masters of the world. I'll sleep with whoever I have to, but you and I always above all the others. We are both a superior race.

And she drank the champagne, savoring it to the very last drop. She sealed the deal by leaning toward him and kissing him on the mouth with the strike of a serpent, thrusting into his throat. Then came a good omen, or was it a divine sign? At that exact moment, the violin fell silent and the sounds of a cheerful orchestra filled the restaurant with the festive melody of "For he's a jolly good fellow, for he's a jolly good fellow, for he's a jolly good fellow… which nobody can deny!" She immediately burst out into a cheerful laugh, throwing her body back with the flexibility of a contortionist and, almost shouting, announcing for all to hear:

— The champagne was to blame!

And Tarud Arab added:

— Bless the champagne!

There was applause, but it was all a mystery. They never knew if it was because the orchestra had decided to make a happy and joyful interruption to silence the tedious whining of the violin or whether it was an expression of jubilation for them. They chose to believe the latter.

Then came the desserts, the dancing, the digestifs and the bill.

— Oooh… it's stratospheric!

— Extra-stratospheric, my little Frenchie.

— Tarud, where did you get that much money?

— There are times when I carry —and winking an eye, he

continued— drugs, my dear. It's just an occasional business, I do not want to raise suspicion.

Having said that, he helped her put on her coat and took the opportunity to whisper into her ear in a subtle, polite and very menacing tone:

— With what I have just told you, you are hopelessly tied to me. You have no way out, Madame Chantal, do you realize how much I trust you, sweetheart?

The wolf had finished his masterly task, and Little Red Riding Hood had definitely gone into the woods.

At last they left. The night was fresh with the scent of springtime. Tarud Arab took a deep breath and exclaimed:

— Nature is our accomplice, look how the night receives us.

As they walked across the red carpet of the restaurant, the boy in uniform who acted as a cicerone at the entrance to the opulent eating place plucked up the courage to say:

— Sir, I believe you left your shoes in the restaurant.

Chapter 14

We arrived and went straight to the shower. We had to clean our bodies and our consciences. Antonieta hugged me as the cool, refreshing water fell upon us. We remained like that for a long time without saying a word. She knew what I was thinking and I knew what she was thinking. We had said "this is my first crime" in a slip of the tongue that had come from us both at almost the same instant and for identical reasons. We were both referring to the second crime we would commit, I against her and she against me. Would fate be a mathematical and pre-established design with intent and malice? Because surely the future death of Fernandísimo Plaza de los Reyes meant either my death or that of Antonieta in the short period subsequent to his departure. Did everything depend on destiny or our criminal talent? I took the soap and began to lather her back.

— Antonieta, what do we do with the bodies?

— Nothing. It's their problem. Let them sort it out.

I was frightened by her response. It was clear that she had more criminal talent than I did.

— But what about the police?

— Don't worry. If they find them you know perfectly well that the dead don't talk.

— But the police investigate. We must have left prints for sure.

— Yeah, but don't worry, we'll find an alibi. Now I want you to make love to me in the shower.

I wasn't expecting that. I simply couldn't do it.

— Antonieta, I'm sorry. I can't. I really can't.

She licked her lips and taking my hand she directed it to her pubis. She began making small moans and undulating movements with her hips.

I still couldn't do it.

— Antonieta, no... there's no way. As much as I want to there's just no way. It won't respond and my head won't either.

I realized that if you want to make love you shouldn't kill a human being just beforehand. It's like when you should never go swimming right after eating, you could get cramp. You kill one of your fellow humans and you get the cramps of frigidity and impotence. I hoped they were temporary symptoms. I concluded that this didn't happen to women. Well, not to Antonieta anyway.

— Ricardo, you're leaving me frustrated. It would have been useful to help me relax.

Considering the tale of terror we had experienced and the crimes we had committed, I thought she was already quite relaxed. Why did she want to be more relaxed?

— I guess we won't tell Fernandísimo.

— Tell him what?

— Antonieta, for God's sake, what do you mean what? We just killed two people!

— Two people who wanted to kill us!

— But that doesn't mean...

— Ah! Anyway I just forgot. Did we kill someone? Ricardo, you're delirious! You and I just got back from a trip to Jupiter. We were abducted by a spacecraft for a while and they brought us back. That's what we'll tell Fernandísimo.

— Antonieta, you're joking!

— No, I'm speaking very seriously. Fernandísimo Plaza de los Reyes is one of those types who swallows any old story like most people on this planet.

— But why should we tell a lie like that! It's absurd.

— It could be an excellent alibi. Haven't you considered it? The more absurd the reasons someone defends, the more respectable people consider them. Convince yourself, Ricardo, we live surrounded by a herd of very stupid sheep.

— Antonieta, what a contemptuous way to consider your fellow humans!

— They're not my fellow humans, Ricky, I...

— Don't call me Ricky, please!

— Whatever, I'm from another planet.

She burst out with a silly giggle.

— I'm from Jupiter. And come on, let's hurry. Let's get dressed and go and visit Fernandísimo. We need to get the information out of him about when he's going to New York. Don't let the prey get away!

She went into the other room while I dried myself with the huge red towel on which appeared what I considered to be the unpleasant face of Che Guevara. Some of Antonieta's preferences were unbearable to me, but I put up with them like a Christ on Calvary. While I was drying my behind thinking that Che might bite me, I wondered to myself whether, after killing her, my little ordeals would come to an end or if a single enormous and devastating one would occur.

She turned and poked her head through the doorway, ordering:

— Hurry up, it's getting late... Ricky.

My God, what a woman! I still wasn't certain whether she deserved to live or die.

Chapter 15

As soon as we entered Fernandísimo's house, we found him sitting in one of his regal armchairs in front of the television; a huge screen with a definition that surpassed sharpness. A young man wielding a broom raised it in a warlike pose and hundreds of other young men behind him did the same with their own brooms, cheering and shouting slogans about a new Chile, free of garbage.

— This is the second time I've seen this guy on TV. I saw him recently when I went past a store window. He was a curious young man. He seems different to the typical politician or activist. But, please, sit down. As always you're welcome.

When he finished saying that last sentence, I had the impression that his dog, Mr. Bob, understood human language and much more, because when Fernandísimo said the word 'welcome', the animal growled, expressing what sounded to me like a sentiment of annoyance and disapproval. I realized that my acuity of perception and my intuition had increased markedly. Was it to do with being abducted to Jupiter?

— My dear Fernandísimo, we have to tell you something that you'll find hard to believe —began Antonieta, winking an eye at me behind the old man's back and glaring at me with a stern look of warning.

— My beautiful lady, I'm willing to believe anything after hearing what someone told me about my destiny. I'm happy!

The words of our wealthy friend gave us a fright. Antonieta gave me a look of surprise and concern and I shot back another just the same. Why so happy? What did he mean by destiny? When we talk about destiny we're preferably referring to our future. Could someone have foretold a good future for him? Depending on how you look at the question, a good future could be death if we believe that death is the way to a better, fuller and eternal life. But those beliefs are increasingly rare. Nowadays we prefer to believe that a good future means that we'll have a long life, unless we're extremely poor and suffering from a very painful and crippling disease. Good heavens, a promise of a long life! And what about his colonic cancer? Had they discovered that the cancer had disappeared by divine magic or something? Antonieta should have been an actress. Seemingly elated, she told him:

— Fernandísimo, how marvelous! Don't tell me they've discovered that you haven't got cancer of the colon anymore!

Before Plaza de los Reyes could answer, Mr. Bob immediately growled. Apparently, the dog could smell the lie with its powerful nose. Mr. Bob could easily be a police dog, I thought.

— I'm sorry, my dear friends, but I can't tell you anything. It's something great, but this isn't the time for you or anyone else to know. The time will soon come when you'll know everything. You deserve to be the first, for sure.

Our friend's answer made us feel worse. In those instants, the shadow of doubt and uncertainty had fallen upon us. Would his intestines still contain the key that would open the doors to wealth for us? And if not, how much longer would we have to wait? And, as a result of this last question, another worry struck me. We'd just had a terrible experience in which we could easily have been killed. So, might we not we die before he did? Anything could happen and the fact that anything could happen made me feel even more anguish and anxiety. Who could ensure that Fernandísimo Plaza de los Reyes was inclined to leave Antonieta and myself as his heirs? Unknown and unexpected relatives can appear at funerals at the last minute or even a few days before death during a person's dying moments. It's usually a bastard son who no one has heard of, even the one accused of being the father, and with all the lawyers and legalisms of the system, he manages to prove that the dying man is his father. Agonizing? Who said that the one who's dying agonizes most? There's sudden death, the fatal heart attack, the tsunami, the earthquake, the terrorist attack, the armed robbery resulting in death! Plaza de los Reyes could well leave this life just like anyone, without any notice and without having put all his affairs in order! I felt an intense burning in my stomach and I started thinking that one couldn't live like this, always expecting something better to improve our lives. In the interim during such a life, you don't live, you suffer.

— Beautiful Antonieta, tell me the incredible thing that you experienced and you said you were going to tell me.

On the TV screen, the handsome young man with the broom, appearing in a close-up where we could see part of the cleaning utensil held against his chest, said phrases like: "What we need is unity of thought, decision and action..."; "...the necessary action is not to confer power on the corrupt who currently exercise it over us; he who has power over me is because I have given it to him..."; "...and in this sense, action is not violence, I condemn violence from every point of view because violence is the power of these corrupt people over honest and decent Chileans"; "...so then, the action to take is not violence but disobedience."

As soon as Antonieta opened her mouth to accede to Fernandísimo's request, she had to close it, as he gestured at her to remain silent; he wanted to hear the guy on the TV. The words of the patriot with the broom –as he was labeled by the captions sliding past under the image– continued: "Violence no, disobedience yes. Compatriots, think: do we take God's power over us by disobeying him, do you realize how serious it is? Did you know that there were times in the life of Jesus when he couldn't perform his healing miracles simply because people didn't believe in Him, didn't have faith in Him and thus they took away the power that Jesus had to heal them? Do you realize how serious it is? And even more serious, Chileans, we don't hesitate to have faith in corrupt politicians with twisted ideologies, proven by history to be failures, and yet we give them the power over us to destroy our quality of life, so they can mock us right in our faces, so they can enjoy the privileges that they grant themselves and allow them to turn Chile into a pile of corruption, ignorance, abuse and criminal and social violence. I urge you to have your wits about you, to DISOBEY so they lose their power and go to hell! All of them will look better at home, I assure you!" Shouts of laughter from the screen.

— An interesting individual that. He seems very inspired. Did you notice that he has something mystical about him?

— Yes —said Antonieta and I nodded my head.

— Well, tell me about this incredible thing that happened to you.

He turned down the volume of the television and prepared to listen.

I thought that Antonieta had repented about telling her crazy lie about the Jupiter abduction, which pleased me greatly. She hesitated, made an unintelligible murmur and then fell silent. The voice of the broom patriot was barely audible with the volume so low and some unexpected barks made by Mr. Bob. Was he telling his master to be careful about the lie Antonieta was about to tell him? I dare say so, because as soon as the dog stopped barking, Antonieta began lying.

— Fernandísimo, weren't you surprised that so many days went by without us coming to visit you?

— No!

Silence.

— Oh, well... anyway... We'd got back from the lake and we were driving to your house in the car because we thought we'd been rude to you to leave you all alone on a weekend without even having warned you, when...

— I'm never all alone...

Another silence.

— ...my faithful Mr. Bob is always with me.

Mr. Bob made himself more comfortable, stretching out in front of Fernandísimo and resting his head on his master's shoes.

— Oh, well, yes... anyway. The thing is that we were going along the road that goes around the lake when suddenly...

I realized that Antonieta was going down the wrong path. If she was going to tell him about having been at the lake and driving on the road around it, her alibi would be nothing of the kind. I decided to intervene.

— Antonieta, something happened to your brain. Maybe they modified it on Jupiter?

Fernandísimo gave a jump and his eyes looked like a pair of fried eggs.

— Honey, it's been such a looong, looong time since we've been to the lake. Remember. We were coming down from the mountains on the road to San José de Maipo. How could you have forgotten?

— Oh, yes, yes... it must have been those beings from Jupiter.

Fernandísimo jumped again, this time with his eyes popping out.

—Well, the thing is that we were coming down there, where Ricardo says, when suddenly there was an intense light, with a clarity, brightness, power and radiance never before seen which blinded us and... boom! We were abducted!

Fernandísimo made a final jump, his eyes like boiled eggs, bulging from their sockets, with his mouth open and tongue out like a hanged man after dropping violently on a rope.

There was a long silence. In the background, very faint, there was still the voice of the broom patriot. When the millionaire's face returned to normal, he asked:

— Jupiter? What do you mean? Is Jupiter the name of some hot springs in the Cajón del Maipo?[5] Is 'abducted' a marketing term they use to talk about spending a season at the hot springs? That seems like ingenious advertising to me.

— No, Fernandísimo. Jupiter is a planet in our solar system.

—- I know, Antonieta, but let's get things straight. I imagine that you aren't telling me that you were abducted in the Cajón del Maipo and that they took you on a little trip to Jupiter. I know there are plenty of UFO sightings in the Cajón del Maipo, but...!

— That's how it was... let Ricardo tell you... the light came, it lifted us up, car and all, then we saw ourselves inside a ship that was very different to the ones in the movies and later we were standing on Jupiter.

—- But how did you know it was Jupiter?

— Well, those beings are like the people from the Rotary Club here. At something that we might understand as an airport, they have a monolith that adopts the language of who whoever's reading it. As soon as I looked at it, the words "Welcome to Jupiter" appeared and immediately under that it said "Service Above Self". They're very advanced, altruistic and civilized.

— Well, well! How did you know that I'm a Rotarian, Antonieta? Only my Rotary friends know that.

— Well... everything's known somewhere, Fernandísimo!

— Ah, yes, ah! Curious! Perhaps tomorrow you'll know how much money I have in the bank.

— Well, that too...

Antonieta suddenly stopped. The excess of spontaneity had almost betrayed her. But the danger had not yet passed.

— Why have you gone quiet? Finish what you started saying, my friend. "That too..." what?

The habit of living in a world of lies makes us quick and nimble when

---

mountain valley just to the southeast of Santiago.

saving situations in which it's necessary, at all costs, to avoid the truth from becoming known. It's a historical endeavor of humanity and Antonieta, of course, is a faithful representative of humanity.

— Well, that also could be possible, I meant. But, by God, Fernandísimo, who would dare to show such disrespect and intrusion!

— Someone very interested in my fortune.

It's not clear to me whether I'm somewhat paranoid, but I had the sensation that Fernandísimo Plaza de los Reyes had very intentionally directed that at us and with a shade of suspicion and irony so we would be very clear that he was no fool. There was another silence in which Antonieta just said, "Ah!" And then another in which nobody moved a muscle until Fernandísimo broke the hush.

— And what do those beings from Jupiter look like?

— Just like us, Fernandísimo, just the same —Antonieta's versatility was astounding— taller in truth. There are men and women and some who seemed to be of a not very well defined third sex from what I could tell. The women are beautiful and the men very attractive and manly. Those of the third sex, let's call them that, were disturbing... and... and... somehow mysteriously exciting... Before them you lose your identity a little... I didn't know whether to become excited as a woman or as a man. It was a very strange experience. The same thing happened to you, didn't it, honey?

— Not exactly, treasure. I was only looking at the women.

— Do you realize, Fernandísimo? Ricardo is a recalcitrant macho. He always boasts that he's a tough billy-goat macho even when we organize those collective erotic experiences that we've told you about and which you've never wanted to attend.

I noticed that Antonieta was enjoying the lie and even as she told it she began to believe it. The truth is that I understood her. Believing what's false is just a matter of words and willingness. It's stated that "in the beginning was the word" and some claim that this world is merely an illusion, a lie. That is to say, the day that God stops talking or writing, will we all disappear?

— You realize what happened to us, Fernandísimo! What do you think? This is big enough to come out in all the newspapers and on television. You have contacts with the press. You could help us sprea the word about our experience. We would be doing science a favor and, incidentally, ourselves. What do you say?

— I say no!

I noticed that Antonieta's charming face changed as her eyes became like a pair of poached eggs.

— No? But why not, my dear friend?

— Because I'm not ready to make a fool of myself. No one is going to believe that story. Even if they do believe it, they wouldn't accept it. Man isn't willing to lose his relevance. Remember what happened to Copernicus.

— But you believe us, right?

— No!

— Nooo!?

— No. It's as if I believed someone who assured me that I'd become the greatest hero of the United States because, thanks to the mental powers I possess and those I've never noticed, I'll provide them with the information on where Osama Bin Laden is hiding.

But, Fernandísimo, that mental power is perfectly possible. Anything can happen in this world.

— I don't think so. You'd have to be stupid to believe it, as stupid as to believe the story of your abduction.

— Are you saying that I'm a liar?

— No, my lovely friend, you're just playing.

— But really, did someone tell you that you had the mental powers to know where Bin Laden is?

— No, no one.

Right away, Plaza de los Reyes took a book, opened it at random and it seemed to me that he was pretending to concentrate on reading it. He sank his head into it. There was a long silence. I felt that between the three of us we all suspected one other.

Chapter 16

L ate at night, Fernandísimo Plaza de los Reyes took slow steps, one-by-one down the interminable staircase that led into the deepest depths of his basement, the third floor underground. There he had assembled a temple with a mixture of pagan and Christian elements. It was a small shrine, his chamber of reflection. That's what he called it to himself, as no one knew of the existence of the place. Unlike the illuminating and decorative paraphernalia in the study of The Psychic of Paris, here the atmosphere was of meditation, intimacy, with dim lighting, soft fragrances, serene figures, static and eternal in time. On what could be called the altar, under the Christian cross —only the cross— was a large and fine mirror framed in gold. In front was an armchair, also gold and upholstered in a fine plush of a regal red. Fernandísimo Plaza de los Reyes sat on it and calmly, with eyelids relaxed, breathing slowly and quietly, and began to look at the image of himself reflected in the mirror. He stayed like that for a long time until the mask on his face began to relax to the point where, almost insensibly, it disappeared. In its place he saw his true face. A calm face, with a sad and deep look, without vestiges of vanity or fear or rage, but with a pristine expression of questioning, of permanent and fundamental questioning. It emerged through his eyes and came from the deepest depths of his heart. I heard him begin to talk and I decided to listen:

— Most High Lord, You who created everything and created me, because You know me, tell me who I am. I think I know that the image in the mirror is nothing but the lie of my being and that I, sat here looking at myself, am another lie of myself. I want to know the Truth. I seek that Truth and it seems that You are trying to hide it from me. Tell me, the world in which we live, is it a truth or is it a lie? What to believe, my God?

I know I have to believe in You, but where are You? What part of this world are You? Or rather, my God, what part of this world is an expression of your existence? Because You are the whole and only truth. What in this world comes from You? Whatever comes from You is part of You and You are You who You are, for just as a drop of water from the ocean contains the whole ocean, so a portion of your being contains your whole being. What is truth and what is a lie on Earth? I want to know to make the right decision, to make sure my steps are on straight paths, to know what to desire and what not to desire, what to do and what not to do. Tell me, Lord of the Most High, Universal Architect of Existence and Life, is it true the power of the powerful on this Earth? Is the majesty of kings, the nobility of princes, the sanctity of the Pope, the power of dictators, the authority of politicians, the justice of judges, the beauty of Miss Universes, the power of money, the prestige of the famous, the balance and the bang of the hammer in Wall Street true? Is the value of money, power and fame authentic? Are they riches that You put in the world so that man could strive for them? Or are they just cravings of the man who gives value to everything that glitters and to everything that makes him appear as important as You? Who is nearest to you? The super-manager sitting in the office on the highest floor of the Empire State Building or the dirtiest of the vagabonds who stumble on the sidewalk covered in filthy rags? Answer me... I hear only your silence... Is your silence an answer? Because if it is I cannot understand it... I'm distressed, Most High, because there is something mysterious that tells me that You exist and that there is a way of being on this earth that fits your desires and your will. A way of being that You look kindly upon. But if I don't know what the Truth is, how will I know what that way of being is like? There's so much noise in this business of life in these parts of the universe that the ears are deafened and we cannot hear You and we become confused. There are so many who speak and preach, those who sing and drum frenetic rhythms, announcers, sellers, promisers, those who present the show, those who provide teaching, those who show you paths, those who tell you what the fashionable achievements are that have to be attained, those who despise you for not attaining those achievements, those who teach you to read one way and write in other. There are so many who speak in your name and they present You with so many different faces that we cannot see You anywhere! And so we cling to lies to believe that they're truths and with those fragile supports we take steps on this earth to fall into the illusion that we're giving the right meaning to our existence. Oh, my Most High, I feel that there's a struggle between You and this world and that has exhausted me. You tell me, since You're supposed to be all-powerful, why do you let the world win in this battle? Or is it that the world isn't beating You and, for wanting to supplant and hide and deny You, we're fatally doomed to total extermination in the end? And is there a never again end or will everything always be an endless comedy of absurdities? Because I can only feel You, but cannot see You or know or understand You. I don't know who I am or where I am or where I have to go. I only invent myself, I guess past roads and I plot future courses. But all this is by obvious worldly influence: I try to be how I'm supposed to be and to advance to where we're all supposed to advance. They teach you that in schools, at universities, in schoolbooks, in philosophical treatises, in symposiums and in lectures, and on television morning shows. But, yours, your divine influence, where is it? Why do You let the prevailing chaos here hide and impede the kingdom of your perfect and serene equilibrium? Or am I wrong in belittling men and myself, thinking that what we want and do contradict your will? For many have also taught that, saying that the words that they have written were dictated by You. How do we know if those who say that are telling the truth or lying? Because at first glance, I see that everything that comes to me comes from the world. Blessed are those who once saw the Virgin or, like Hamlet, the ghost of his father! But those who claim to have seen the Virgin, how do we know if they're lying? And Hamlet who saw the ghost of his father is but another ghost like his own father, created by the imagination of some liar called Shakespeare. Tell me, how are these things? Again your silence in response... To believe or not to believe? And if to believe, believe in what? Only in your silence?

It was neither the time nor moment to break the silence. It was fair and necessary that Fernandísimo Plaza de los Reyes should continue to ask questions. He himself couldn't yet realize that he had already advanced many steps with his constant questions. Not the absolutes, but the necessary ones. When the comic leaves the comedy and is locked in his dressing room and looks at the mirror, he realizes that his face is painted and only then does he begin to return to the origin. Fernandísimo Plaza de los Reyes began talking again:

"Most High Architect, please look at me. How do You see me? I want to tell You how I see myself. Let me laugh! I see myself acting on the worldly stage like a crazy old man, foolish and ridiculous, like a whimsical, eccentric millionaire, but in the end nothing original because my eccentricities are but singular and theatrical expressions of the same tired ambitions, efforts and twisted dreams that every man in humanity has. From the loneliness of here where I am, the world out there looks like a masquerade of imbeciles. Explain to me, High One, why do I want to die in New York when the place where one dies makes no difference? Where does that foolishness come from that a corpse buried in Arlington Cemetery in the United States has more honor than one buried in the General Cemetery in Santiago de Chile? And where does it come from, that thought that one corpse has more status than another, and where does it come from that stupidity of giving importance to the status of a dead person? Is it that there is vanity not only in life, but also in death? There are pits dug to cover bodies that no one claims and there are also graves covered with dirt with at least one wooden cross, which tells us that the dead person isn't much better than an anonymous corpse; then come the concrete niches with cement front covers for those with some status and then the ones with front covers of marble or some similar material for the dead of the middle-middle or upper-middle class. At the top are the regal mausoleums of marble and select stones, with sculptures and sophisticated architecture, with bronzes that display words about the virtues and the importance of the majestic, venerated and deceased fat cat. I say, between the sorrow and laughter that it causes me; in battles so many die and all fighting with equal courage and yet the statues and beautiful mausoleums are only for the generals and captains. What about the hundreds of unknown soldiers, why are there no statues or mausoleums for each of those brave men? What kind of dead person do I want to be? It scares me because I realize that I don't want to settle for being buried in a Carrara marble mausoleum because I'm a rich man, but now I have the strong desire to die as a hero in the United States, given the military honors of that powerful nation and sharing a funerary neighborhood with President J.F. Kennedy and so many others of historic renown. My God, I seem to have started having pharaonic desires! Will it be me, Master? Or is it because of that famous Psychic of Paris...? No, you don't have to answer me. I know about your silence. I think I have the answer. In any case, it's me. Look, Most High, how I see myself in that mirror. Talking about these things, I've put my clown face on again... I can't stop laughing! Hahaha... I'm bursting with laughter...! Excuse me, my Lord! I'm sure You have a sense of humor, right?"

Fernandísimo's question was so naive. One could see that he wasn't entirely convinced of what he was saying. If he had have been, he would have known that I laugh out loud every time I look at them. With the free will I gave them, they have made their world such a hilarious comedy! But I don't laugh to mock, I laugh to enjoy myself. After all, I know that all this is nothing but a soap bubble.

After having burst out laughing for a long while from looking into his pretentious mirror, when Fernandísimo Plaza de los Reyes finally emerged from his third basement to the scene of his everyday activities he didn't even notice when he had the mask on again. There was an overpowering spring wind outside and it was the wind that took away the words that he had directed at me.

Chapter 17

"According to the meteorological report of the Chilean Navy, a storm with winds of up to 90 kilometers per hour is forecast for the evening due to an unexpected and sudden weather front from the Andes. Experts say that..."

— Turn off the radio. It's time to go to the Municipal Theater.

— How strange, Tarud. How can they forecast a storm when there's bright sunshine? What is going on with the weather?

— I don't give a shit what is going on with the weather. What matters to me is that you appear at the Municipal Theater like the Queen of Sheba. Tonight the diva will have to be you and not the prima donna of the opera. Hurry up, it is getting late. We have to deal with the goddamned traffic in this city!

It would be unfair to say that Simone Chantal had no scruples in her upward drive for money and fame. Of course she did, but she kept them very much to herself. The time when she was finally forced to offer her body to the three television producers at the same time, she felt that she was dirty, a vulgar whore, a deteriorated, decaying being, undeserving of forgiveness. She cried as she gave herself to those three unrestrained beasts and she continued crying much later when they had left her alone in the dark room of that house located who knew where, with her head bowed between her knees, her exhausted legs bent and her long hair cascading forward. It was convulsive sobbing. But, after all, her scruple only manifested itself in that. At no point did it slow down her plan and the consolation came later when she learned from a euphoric and triumphant Tarud Arab that the project for the television program had been accepted. Her sense of guilt disappeared as she saw a bright future within reach and almost at hand. That future was gradually becoming a present in which people began asking for autographs in the street, in which the press surrounded her, photographed and filmed her every time she appeared in public, where various municipalities awarded her the title of "The Woman of the Good Omens for Chile" after it was first granted to her by the Ministry of the Interior. Of course, this point deserves to be mentioned with absolute objectivity. This is how it happened. Madame Chantal had attended a gala at the Municipal Theater in Santiago where George Bizet's opera Carmen was playing with an international cast. The well-known psychic had always hated opera, but Tarud Arab, forming a tight chorus with the producers of the television program, obliged her to attend. The ratings, although quite high and very profitable, still hadn't reached the absolute peak expected. The money bag is never full, it's elastic. It was important to be seen at high-status social and cultural events. It was essential to show the sheep that the fortuneteller wasn't just some crazy woman from an obscure background, but a lady of great nobility, of high culture and select social circles. Like everything else, it was a matter of image; something very similar to the white clothes of doctors with a stethoscope hanging from the neck or the dark sunglasses with Italian frames and bronzed complexion of the attention-seekers in show business. She was another puppet in that show, only with a more exotic and bizarre mask that wasn't as tired and conventional as the tanned skin and smoked lenses. She attended the opera in a very long dress that ended in a tail that writhed like a snake as she walked. The dress in question seemed to split her body vertically in two. One half was a dark red garnet color like the stage curtain of a prestigious theater and the other was pitch black. The dress opened at the front in a generous neckline and the rear had a large opening that showed Simone's naked back with enticing freckles that, to many, made her skin more desirable. His arms were also naked and long, with a white and delicate complexion. The shoes had very fine golden stilettos and flashes of crystals. Her head and the lower half of her face were covered with a very fine silk handkerchief, evoking Muslim custom. Nevertheless, on her chest, hanging from her neck on a prominent gold chain, was a large cross, also in gold, like that of the Templar Knights. From the wrist and well up above the forearm there were a variety of bracelets, from which hung figurines such as pyramids, skulls, small beings of demonic appearance, angels and cherubs and some objects of Masonic symbology, such as the compass, square and triangle with an eye in the middle, as well as motifs related to Eastern religions such as Buddhism, Hinduism and others. Her arms bore an openly ecumenical and inclusive spirit. The Madame herself was an even more striking spectacle than the opera. So it was thus that, during the intermission and in the foyer of the theater, where there was a buffet with delicacies and good liquor, the press and TV people filmed her, photographed her, televised her, and everyone asked her for autographs, wanted to appear by her side, praised her for her exoticism and beauty, for her powers of divination and for her charm. No one commented on the first act of the opera. The topic was Madame Chantal, The Psychic of Paris, live, direct and in person. Someone there, a forty-odd year old man who bragged about being familiar with operas and insisted on telling everyone that he had seen the great divas at none other than the Milan Scala for four seasons and for three more seasons at the Metropolitan Opera House of New York, stated with absolute certainty that Madame Chantal had a voice with immense lyrical potential and that, along with fortunetelling, she should dedicate herself to "bel canto" and become a soprano of international fame. The boasts of the man reached the ears of the diva of divination, who thanked him from afar with a smile and an expression in her eyes that came from the womb. The forty-year-old couldn't believe it and, emboldened, he moved toward her, ready to make her his prey. Who would have said that he would end up in bed with The Psychic of Paris! But he was forced to abort the operation. Just at that moment a man of devastating looks interposed; the very essence of elegance, of masculine beauty, seldom seen at his advanced and perfectly preserved years, and with a dominating demeanor capable of overpowering any situation. The opera fan shrank and backed away with his tail between his legs. It was thus that the madame saw a mature gentleman of tall stature come to within just a few inches of her, with his venerable gray hair and a silver-handled stick, which helped him conceal a slight limp and, in passing, accentuated his air of distinction. With a smile that Clark Gable himself would envy, he said:

— Distinguished lady, grant me the pleasure of allowing me to introduce myself. I am Patricio Guzmán Peralta, Confidential Advisor to the Minister of Culture.

Tarud Arab, who was beside Simone at that moment, stepped away discreetly to allow the counselor to be alone with his Psychic of Paris.

The flamboyant Madame Chantal, The Psychic of Paris, slightly inclined her face, which was made up as if for a Hollywood production of the fifties by the famous Luis Patricio. That tilt was a gesture of subtle coquetry. Careful to pronounce each word with academic clarity and imitating the tone of the well-to-do people of the country, she replied:

— Oh! It is an honor for me that you introduce yourself to me, Mr. Guzmán!

— Guzmán Peralta, my beautiful lady —corrected the high-ranking government official with a benevolent smile.

— Sorry, I tend to be distracted in the present due to concentrating so much on the future.

To Simone her excuse seemed marvelous. She showed ingenuity and professionalism. She felt satisfied with herself. To Guzmán Peralta it sounded like a corny and idiotic response and he wondered if perhaps he wasn't being more stupid than her for accepting the mission that he had to accomplish with that woman. It comforted him to see that at least she projected a sparkling image of exotic beauty. Intoxicated with that image he replied:

— I understand the seriousness of your business, Madame. It is incredible that a woman like you, possessor of a beauty radically different from any other and even greater than all others, is destined to dive into the depths of existence of past times, into the future and in this random present in which we live.

Guzmán Peralta had listened to his own words and was very satisfied with both himself and his speech. The madame found him pretentious and boring. She replied:

— I am flattered by your profound words and I thank you, Mr. Guzmán.

— Guzmán Peralta! —This time without a smile.

— How stupid of me! Forgive me once again. As I already said, because of concentrating so much....

— I know, madam, you look into your crystal ball so much that when you stop you cannot see the things around you quite so clearly.

There was an awkward silence. Simone wondered if this was a rude irony or a direct insult regarding her lack of intelligence. What was she really, intelligent or stupid? Guzmán Peralta felt that he had made an error. The defense of his lineage was undermining the success of his mission. So he poured her a glass of champagne, raised his and said "cheers", looking her in the eye with an enthralled face. They drank. Simone's energetic deglutition, untrained for such high-class occasions, caused her embarrassment. Her swallowing sounded as grotesque and unfortunate as a high C bellowed out of time and out of tune. Guzmán Peralta decided that he should ignore every dissonant note and get to the point as soon as possible. The intermission was not long and at the very least he had to get down to business in that lapse of time.

— Distinguished Madame Simone Chantal, let me cut to the chase. I am here to talk to you not only at the behest of the Minister of Culture, but also on behalf of the Ministry of the Interior and, ultimately, the Presidency of the Republic itself.

Simone's chin dropped slightly. From a distance, a smile of mischief and complicity came to the eyes of Tarud Arab, who was watching and pretending not to. Guzmán Peralta took Simone's arm very gently and led her towards a corner that was somewhat secluded, for a thick curtain of garnet red plush concealed anyone who was there. Something else came to Simone's mind.

— No, please, Madame, do not think ill of me. You are beautiful and very attractive, but I am a gentleman. We need to speak about this far from... shall we say... the madding crowd. What I am here to say and propose is a state secret and involves the highest interests of the nation.

Simone Chantal gulped... to herself.

— Let's get down to business. I know, and all of us in the government believe that you are a serious psychic and that you don't lie. Your successes are astounding. But my question is; would you be willing to lie?

The Psychic of Paris didn't delay even a millionth of a second in responding.

— No, certainly not!

— I expected that answer, of course. But, Madame, think, sometimes lies are necessary. For example, not telling the whole truth, only a part of it, is certainly one way of lying. Viewed thus, God can be considered something of a liar, for He has revealed to men only a small part of the Truth. It means that this lie is necessary to protect a greater good.

— Well, of course. Nevertheless…

— And think too of a war. The enemy must hide information from their enemy and deceive them. Lying is a part of military tactics. You realize, camouflage itself is a lie. But that lie can serve to save one's life and…

— And it can also serve to take the lives of others, correct?

— Well, no doubt. What I want to say is that lying is not always bad. Pious lies are necessary to avoid greater evils on many occasions. We would like to invite you to participate with us in a pious lie that will do the country a great deal of good.

Concealed by the thick drapery, they both heard a group pass by, laughing rather stridently. That was somewhat strange in that environment, thought Guzmán Peralta. He suddenly wondered, did they hear me? He waited for the revelers to move away and returned to his task.

— Madame, what do you say?

— What do you want me to say, Mr. Guzmán?

— Guzmán Peralta!

— Oh yes! Guzmán Peralta.

— I pray you do not refuse the government what the government requests of you. We appeal to your patriotism.

— I am French, Mr. Guzmán Peralta.

— But you have lived in Chile for many years. More than anything you have been the beneficiary of this beautiful country. We know a lot about you, believe me… — He paused deliberately and fixed his gaze on her without moving a muscle in his face; then continued in a soft, friendly, warm tone— …and we admire you greatly, believe me.

Simone tried to gain a clear understanding of everything that was happening to her, but her mind didn't seem to be working too well. She was confused and felt the need for Tarud Arab to be there. She could not, did not know how to decide for herself. She had started out as a puppet of the TV show production team. But although they had already turned her into a marionette (I am merciful), a flash inside her brain suddenly seemed to inspire her: if the whole program was nothing but a mess of lies, taking advantage of the naivety, credulity, ignorance and stupidity of the masses that won her the ratings, how would it be to lie with the backing of none other than the government of the nation! What thief would refuse to steal if they were protected by the law, as it is indeed usually done? And besides, behind all this there would have to be some profit.

— Yes, Mr. Guzmán Peralta, I agree to lie if the government of Chile needs me to do so and if it is for the greater good of society. Please tell me the details.

The confidential advisor to the culture minister squinted his eyes for a second and then looked at her, pleased.

— In as few words as possible, Madame, the matter is as follows: You know as well as we do that when a large mass of citizens opposes the legitimately established government and loses confidence in the authorities, that does the country no good at all from any perspective. We have to acknowledge that we, as a government, have made some mistakes, more by hurried handling of certain issues than for any more serious reason. We also acknowledge that we have had cases of corruption, but they are isolated cases, believe me. Well, the truth is that this has caused social and political discontent and, worst of all, mistrust. This last point is serious. Distrust can lead to disobedience, then rebellion and even the dissolution of authority, and then chaos ensues.

Simone put on a serious face. She frowned to show concern, but to herself she realized that she understood little or nothing and that, deep down, none of this mattered to her. Guzmán Peralta continued.

— In short, what we want you to do is to state during your television program that, according to your divinatory science, there are excellent omens for government administration and, as a consequence of that, a bright future for the country.

The fortuneteller thought to herself and then said:

— But, Mr. Guzmán Peralta, my job is not based on lies. I would not know how to lie about political issues and matters like that. The truth is that I don't know how to lie at all on any subject. I was educated in a fervently Catholic family in France and from a young age I was taught that lying was a sin that offended God greatly.

Inwardly, the confidential advisor burst out into a guffaw that certainly no one had heard and, very seriously, he said:

— We will advise you constantly. We will tell you what you have to say. And, believe me, deep down what we ask is not that you lie. Consider it simply as a communicational strategy to help the country regain confidence in its authorities. I am also a believer, I was a seminarian when I was young, but God had reserved another place for me on this earth; to be a public servant, someone who works for the social welfare of the people and the oppressed. I assure you that God will look favorably upon your collaboration.

Simone also burst out laughing inwardly. For her, God was no more than a simple word that, when spoken, could give a certain believability to others.

— The reward for your services will be monthly payments for a year of worthy and not inconsiderable fees such as you deserve, in addition to an award from the ministries of the Interior and Culture consisting of an honorary title that will give you status, prestige and national historicity. How does that sound?

Simone's eyes glittered and bubbles of happiness filled her head. She replied:

— The reward offered is great, but even greater and more important is the conviction that I will be serving this, my second country. I agree!

Guzmán Peralta took her softly by the elbow and they came out from behind the curtain. Outside the gong had already sounded to announce that the intermission had ended. As soon as Tarud Arab saw them, he came closer.

— Madame Chantal is a great lady —said Guzmán Peralta.

Tarud Arab understood everything. He responded with a slight nod.

— Until we meet again, Madame Chantal. We will be in touch sooner than you think.

— I hope so. See you soon, Mr. Guzmán.

— Guzmán Peralta!

The sounds of the opera and the high Cs resumed. The splendid and shining costumes, the masks, the makeup, excellent choreography, the expression of bodies, harmony and beauty in the lighting, the majestic and beautiful fantasy in the designs and scenery. On the stage emerged an ideal world from the depths of human creativity. Nevertheless, Tarud Arab's desires were being fulfilled to his complete satisfaction. Observing the behavior of the public, he saw how many of them focused their eyeglasses on the striking lady seated beside him, the famous Madame Chantal. But it was not only those with eyeglasses who observed her, ignoring the comings and goings on the stage, but also the spectators watching with the naked eye. Many of them continually turned to look at the balcony where the madame and her manager were seated. At a moment when the soprano, displaying her beautiful art, ended an aria with a high note that would be historic and which the public rewarded with spontaneous, euphoric and generous applause, what would be unthinkable to any sane mind took place. A spotlight, directed by who knows who, shone on The Psychic of Paris who, standing up, was applauding enthusiastically. The attention of everyone was focused on her balcony and the applause that had originally been for the prima donna was eventually all directed at the prima diviner of Paris and the TV channel 24 breakfast show.

— You have won, my sweet. You are the Queen of Sheba —whispered Tarud Arab.

— I know —she replied, smiling at the audience and blowing kisses from afar.

The opera resumed and this time it felt like it was slipping towards the end. Without explaining it to themselves, the audience saw how, from this point onward, the cast seemed angry with one other, even in the love duets. The soprano's voice no longer seemed the same, it seemed hoarse, as if she were scraping her throat when she sang and, at the end, when the unloved lover murders Carmen, at the moment before the fatal stab, she shouted "*laisse-moi passer*" at her attacker with a tone of such hatred and vulgarity that it resembled more the rude cry of a market trader than a dramatic warning and supplication from the lips of a sublime artist of the stage. And, to boot, the final blow was not the spiteful and painful attack of a jealous lover, thrusting his blade into the belly of his beloved with a Toledan steel dagger, but rather a brutal slash administered by Jack the Ripper with a butcher's knife. Nonetheless, the last fall of the curtain was greeted with frenetic applause and, once again, a persistent person directed a spotlight at the balcony hosting Madame Chantal, the now polemic Psychic of Paris. She stood up once more and rivaled the stage performers with her bows and smiles. It turned into a battle of blessings, smiles and kisses blown into the air from the stage by the actors and from the box by the diva of divination, and the public, crazed by this unexpected contest, transformed the applause into thunderous noise that roared in a mad crescendo alternately towards the stage and the balcony. There was a pandemonium of clapping, bravos, whistles and laughter. Mouths opened, eyes were shot with blood, hair became disheveled and hands flapped like furious pigeons. The musical box that the Municipal Theater has always been became a cavern of noises from hell. To be there was to have fallen into the depths of madness. But all of a sudden the noise suddenly stopped. A huge, booming sound exploded outside. It was a wild roar of nature that paralyzed everyone. There was absolute silence, a silence filled with fear. Two far more powerful crashes were felt. No one moved the slightest muscle. And then, each and every one began to hear how the rain started falling on the roof of the theater. Soft and light at first, but then with calamitous fury. This was no longer mere rain, but a dreadful deluge. In those instants, many thought that what they had heard was the end of days, that the Apocalypse was drawing near, nature was beginning to take her revenge. Men often blame me for their negative tendencies. Things got worse when they felt as if the entire ocean was falling onto the roof and then, when they saw that the rain was penetrating the ceiling and began to fall thick, heavy and dense onto the stage and the stalls, it was no longer a mere feeling, but was evident. There were waterfalls, buckets of water flooding the theater and it seemed to be going down with almost the same fate as the supposedly unsinkable Titanic. The screaming began, the cries of horror and the entire cast of famous artists and the select and numerous audience of opera aficionados became a horde of savages who ran wild, crashing into each other, pushing one another and trampling the fallen, each thinking only of saving their own skin. It was only Tarud Arab who was not thinking solely of himself. Both he and Simone needed to be saved. "You mean a lot to my life," he shouted as he took her by the hand and she, flattered, allowed herself to be dragged, knee deep through the water, out to the street. Outside, the curtain of water meant nothing could be seen. There were the rumbling crashes of thunder, the honking of car horns and occasional crashes between them, and the night was suddenly and violently lit up by the instantaneous and electrifying illumination of lightning bolts. Thanks to one of those explosions from the sky, Madame Chantal's legs turned to jelly and she fell heavily to the ground. Contrary to what she expected, Tarud Arab did not stop to pick her up. Separated from her hand, he continued in his crazed escape to anywhere. At this point, given the apocalyptic circumstances, he had forgotten value of profit. The Psychic of Paris, on all fours in a pool of water and lashed by a true deluge, had become flotsam, a wet and beaten cat with a pale face and no sign of makeup, arms without bracelets and neck without necklaces. The Templar cross sank into a muddy puddle and the bracelets and rings were carried away by streams of water that flowed like unrestricted rivers, ignoring sidewalks, corners, or municipal regulations. In her quadrupedal position, soaked hair sticking to her face, her features washed to the very last and most intimate wrinkle, she imagined herself as a naked witch on a broomstick but unable to fly and sinking into the torrent of raging waters. Then she whispered to herself, "My name is Simone Chantal and I'm not even sure of that." From the heavens, a thunderclap seemed to answer her with a powerful boom of approval.

Chapter 18

Do men enjoy or suffer the right of free will? It has its risks, so it isn't good to choose to be in the wrong place at the wrong time. That was what happened to poor Johnny Tunante. He had had the idea of wandering around the foothills of the mountains close to Santiago, before stumbling across a half-burned truck and verifying that inside were two charred corpses, one evidently with an large skeleton, the other somewhat smaller. It had also occurred to him to dig into the mouth of the big one and pull out a gold tooth, blackened by the fire. And so it happened that he ran into the police with his hands in the cookie jar, so to speak.

Johnny Tunante, fatherless as far back as he could remember, grew up with his mother spending most of his time in the cemetery. She, Otilia, earned a living by tending to the tombs and graves in the General Cemetery, while baby Johnny spent the time beside her surrounded by gravestones, crosses and flower arrangements in a shoebox padded with an old, worn blanket that she used as a cradle. His childhood consisted almost entirely of accompanying his mother day after day in those funereal surroundings, while his adolescence was spent learning that there were people who desecrated tombs to steal from the deceased, in complicity with his mother who received a small recompense for looking the other way and allowing the thefts to take place. With such a teaching, that became his way of earning pocket money. Stealing from the dead was far less risky than robbing the living. Of course, he was never going to earn a hundred years of forgiveness[6] because, as far as we know, the dead don't steal.

---

[6] This refers to a popular refrain in Chile, *Quien roba a un ladrón, tiene cien años de perdón* – He who robs a thief has a hundred years of forgiveness.

For some reason that the high-ranking authorities of the police might want to forget, it had been a long time since any officers had been sent to patrol the wilderness of the Andean foothills. More a matter of image than anything else, they had opted to assign virtually all the resources of the mounted police to show off in the streets of the capital rather than to supervise rural and mountainous zones. Therefore, the appearance of a patrol car in this area was an unusual thing and something that could be considered part of Johnny Tunante's karma. Nothing in anyone's life happens by mere chance.

— Sir, do you see what I see?

— How do I know what you're seeing, Carrasco? Are we soul mates?

— No, but you're looking ahead just like me, sir, with all due respect.

— I can't see anything.

— Perhaps you should leave the pretense aside, sir. I think it's time for you to wear glasses. With respect.

— There's no need to get cocky, Carrasco. I can see perfectly well. There's the burned remains of what looks to have been a truck.

— Yes, and…

— But, look, let's turn a blind eye to it. We haven't seen it. We're about to end the shift and I've got no desire for it to go on any longer. If we start an inspection, just think about the time that we'll finish. Let's go back.

— You see you can't see?! There's a man there crouching over something and he seems to be struggling.

The officer made a gesture of resignation. If there was a suspect they couldn't turn back. He ordered Carrasco to drive the car right up to the scene. When Johnny Tunante saw that the police were beside him, he raised both hands, although no one was pointing a gun at him.

— These guys have been dead for a while. I had nothing to do with it, off… officer.

— We'll see about that. What were you doing crouching down there? —The officer stared at him.

— I was taking a tooth from one of the deceased, off… officer.

— So it wasn't enough just to kill them, but also you rob your victims once you've finished them off.

Johnny Tunante jumped back and hid behind the carcass of the pickup, then poked his head out cautiously, replying:

— I never killed anyone. I swear. And I wasn't stealing. Taking a tooth from a dead man, even if it is gold, isn't robbery. Is that tooth going to be useful to someone who's dead? What's the point of taking riches to the grave if it's for nothing? Meanwhile, I'm alive and kicking. I believe that when someone dies they stop being selfish. Don't you think, off... officer?

Corporal Carrasco spoke to the suspect for the first time.

— Speak up slowly. Why did you kill these two people and then burn them with the truck and everything?

— I already told you. I had nothing to do with this terrible business. I was passing by and I found this and took the opportunity. Whenever I see a dead man I take whatever he's wearing. I take everything from him so that he can go to heaven nice and light. I do a favor for the dead and the dead does one for me. Haven't you heard what the priest says? "It's more difficult for a camel to pass through the eye of a needle than a rich man to get through the gates of heaven." You have to get to heaven buck naked, if not, Saint Peter throws you back with a kick up your ass. I don't hurt anyone, off... officers.

The cops looked at each other and laughed. They had a real clown before them and at the same time the culprit of a horrendous murder. Case solved. A point scored for them.

The prosecutor arrived at the scene of the crime, as well as the detectives, the people from the forensics lab, etcetera, etcetera, and the press. There was a photo of the monster on the front pages of the newspapers, television footage of the jackal taken from angles that made him look intimidating. They had a culprit so they were all excited, they were happy, there was someone to focus all their fury on, all their hatred, all the aggression in that pressure cooker called Chilean society. But justice had not yet been done. He was just the accused. Let's see at the results of the investigation. What investigation? Not on your life! This guy is the killer, it's obvious! We'll soon see how the courts declare him guilty and give him the right sentence! The bad thing about this country is that there's no death penalty anymore! They should reinstate it and kill this guy in some way that makes him suffer slowly. Some Chinese torture. Just imagine, the victims were two humble workers, with families, with small children, hardworking and decent people who had bought that truck after a lot of work and saving. They were well liked in their neighborhood because of their friendliness and generosity, for giving children religious or moral lessons, all without charging; they were evangelicals. Some people disputed this. No, they were devout Catholics, humble, but good people. The controversy surrounding them spread. Other religions also claimed them. Rabbi Perez Calderón claimed that both had Jewish Sephardic ancestry. The Muslim community also spoke out. The rabbi was lying. The victims were clearly Palestinian. Just how far would the Jews go to claim anything belonging to Palestine! The Jewish community replied that the only one of Palestinian origin was Johnny Tunante, a false name of course to hide his true identity. There were comments that the guy had links with Al Qaeda and that he had tried to bring Muslim terrorism to South America starting with Chile. The press lapped up all the controversy and the circulation of the newspapers tripled and the ratings of the television newscasts rose far above their historic peaks. The young activist with the broom on his shoulder stopped appearing in the media. In light of all this he wasn't news at all and his cause meant little to most. He organized a march on the Alameda[7] with his followers and from a platform he claimed that that terrible finger of accusation against Johnny Tunante was nothing more than a montage by the ruling elite to distract attention from the serious problems that were affecting the country due to corruption, poor administration and misgovernment. Apart from his followers only a few people congregated in front of the stage. They had to get home in time to watch the soap opera that was doing so well and, of course, see the news about the evil jackal and arsonist. The young patriot's speech wasn't covered by television, the press or the radio. Only his supporters took pictures with their phones.

During his pre-trial detention, Johnny Tunante was allowed to watch TV because the prison warden's father was buried in a niche in the General Cemetery and he knew Otilia, Johnny's mother, who cared for and decorated that particular niche with special care. So the jackal, the current flavor of the month, saw everything that was said and shown about him. Johnny was fascinated. He was the center of attention of the whole country. No one had ever even noticed him before. He felt happy, but he wondered: "Why so much fuss about me just because I took a gold tooth from a dead man?"

---

[7] The main avenue in Santiago, which crosses the center of the city, east-west.

Chapter 19

Dialogue behind closed doors. But that doesn't work with me. There isn't the slightest thing that shall not be known.

— If we want to proceed ethically and fairly, as is appropriate, it's necessary to clarify the facts and prove whether he was the murderer or not.

— That involves an exhaustive forensic investigation. It would be essential to allocate a large amount of resources and sufficient time.

— That's right. It's the only way.

— That's where the problem begins.

— How do you mean?

— Are you naïve or are you after the Nobel Prize for Justice?

—You offend me, Minister.

— No, I'm being objective.

— But really I can't believe that you...

— You can believe or disbelieve whatever you want. Understand this, we're short of funds, a lot has been stolen and continues to be stolen. There are interests that can't be touched and we have to be austere in fiscal spending if we want don't want to touch those interests and continue stealing. While I wouldn't call it theft, it's simply collecting more than is unfairly established by the law for services to the country that demand work without schedules, leaving the family aside, being exposed to becoming a victim at any time in an attack and suffering the erosion of our personal image as a consequence of the biased propaganda of the media and our opponents.

— I hadn't thought of it that way, Minister.

— That's because you don't think.

— Minister, I...

— On the other hand, the public desperately needs to see concrete facts that the authority imposes authority, punishes the criminal and administers justice. It has been too long that we have left the criminals to do as they like due to populist and electoral reasons convenient to ourselves. We have given them a kind of haven and that haven for them means new votes for us. But it's time for a different gesture. Public opinion or the rabble demands it because they feel insecure, they're talking about misrule, about chaos. It's time to show them that the government has not set aside the iron fist. We'll call it justice to avoid making any allusion or establishing any relationship with the Pinochet dictatorship. That Johnny Tunante is a gift from God. Guilty or not, he will be found guilty. The judges have already been spoken to. The congressmen and senators have also been spoken to. The law will be amended quickly in a manner appropriate to these circumstances and the death penalty will be restored. The media have also been spoken to and will invent the worst possible past for that Tunante and the most tender and Catholic past for the victims burned in the truck. They will be portrayed as two people who are now most certainly seated at the right hand of God. So when it's announced that Johnny Tunante was found guilty and that he will consequently receive the maximum penalty, which will consist of execution by lethal injection, everyone will be happy and everybody will applaud us ecstatically. Our ratings will rise much higher.

— But Minister, what you telling me sounds something like...

— It can sound however it likes to you. That won't stop the system. If you go on like this, it would be better for you not to work with us anymore and return to the anonymity and insignificance of the rabble. You can see that you've never read Machiavelli. It's the bible of every powerful man.

— I don't want to go back to the rabble, Minister. I promise to read the man with the Italian surname.

— That sounds good. I'll give you a copy, and after you've read it, we'll talk.

— Very kind of you, Minister. Minister, just one thing, forgive me. I understand that before the death penalty was carried out by firing squad. So why lethal injection?

— If we reinstate the death penalty we have to show that we're moving with the times, that we're charitable and that we know how to economize on resources.

— I understand, Minister. Very clever of you... So everyone has been spoken to.

— Not only spoken to, but also with promise of a generous reward. Everything is assured.

— Generous reward!

— Yes, Espinoza, a generous reward...! Espinoza, a piece of advice.

— Yes, Minister.

— I like you in spite of everything. That's why I'm giving you this advice: Follow me, stick beside me, serve me loyally and... you will become rich, I can assure you!

— Thank you, Minister... thank you... thank you very much.

— Go away now.

— Yes, yes, Minister.

On leaving the meeting, Espinoza was already someone else. For the moment, I had one less sheep in my flock. At least there on Earth.

Chapter 20

As soon as I hung up the phone, out of pure joy I took off my moccasins and threw them into the air, yippeeee! I rushed to our bedroom, yelling Antonieta's name.

— Antonieta, it's happening!

— Has that Johnny Tunante been convicted that for crime we committed?

— Something better than that.

— Could there be anything better than that?

— Definitely. Fernandísimo wants us to go and see him at once. He's anxious. He says that we should see him right now and that he's decided to go to New York.

— But...

— No buts about it. Get dressed quickly and let's go. Opportunities have to be taken instantly or they're lost.

— What opportunity?

— To get rich, stupid.

Antonieta fumbled in the closet. She flung skirts, blouses, shoes, sneakers, jackets, and whatever clothes she had into the air. And like a stripper desperate to go on stage, she threw on the clothes that were closest to hand and ran after me, as I was already out of the door. She followed me, brushing and tidying her hair. We were already on the sidewalk when I had to go back. I ran to my desk and put on my moccasins and sped off again like a lunatic. I'd realized that it would've been very painful to speed up and slow down without shoes and even more embarrassing when the socks had a hole in the big toe. Antonieta never agreed to cut my nails. Old-fashioned women were much more industrious. My mother always did it when I was single. I was always a very pampered child until I was thirty.

We arrived, went in, greeted him and got straight to the point.

— Fernandísimo, what made you decide what you decided to decide?

I used flowery language for his pleasure, to show that I also had Spanish ancestry, which worked wonders with the tongue of Cervantes. And he answered me like he was carrying out a matador's pass on a bull.

— What made me decide what I decided to decide was television and gratitude.

There was a short pause. I was waiting. I thought that it could've done with a final *olé*!

— With all due respect, I don't understand —said Antonieta.

Fernandísimo gave her a look. He looked her up and down from head to toe and winked.

— There's a surprise for you, girl. A very good one.

Then he addressed me in a good-natured tone.

— And also for you of course, my young friend.

Then he leaned forward and took both of us by the hands.

— I am very grateful to you. You have offered me friendship, company, affection, concern. Very few people do that with an old man. Usually the old are isolated because they're considered a hindrance.

— But not rich old men like you.

It was too late. Antonieta's excess spontaneity and enthusiasm had begun to ruin everything. Mr. Bob, always sitting beside his master, gave a growl. The animal definitely understood. When he was alone with Fernandísimo, did he speak the language with him? I thought my idea wasn't so far-fetched. I remembered that, in the Bible, the donkey on which Balaam was riding said to him, "Balaam, what have I done to you to make you beat me?" And, as far as I know, the Bible doesn't lie. Or does it?

Antonieta turned as red as a tomato and was about to begin apologizing when Fernandísimo interrupted her. He got up from his chair and picked up a cane with a gold handle. He brandished it menacingly in front of us. We recoiled, aghast.

— That's enough! Your mask has slipped, sweetheart! And you, young man, get her out of here now because I know perfectly well what's behind yours. Get out of here both of you right now!

Mr. Bob made three clear, concise, authoritative and threatening barks. Clutching on to each other, we shrank away in shock to the door, which was closed. We tried to open it, but our clumsiness, induced either by fear or some latch keeping it shut, prevented us from doing so. Worst of all, Mr. Bob had rushed at us and was barking, showing us his fangs. He had us trapped between his ferocious canine inheritance of wolves and the complicity of the damned door. Farther back, Fernandísimo Plaza de los Reyes, converted into a righteous knight-errant and avenger, wielded his cane, pointing it at Antonieta and I, who at that precise moment were wishing that we had never coveted the fortune of that angry rich man. It's not a good idea to offend a rich man, unless you know that your crime will go unpunished. I remembered those two bastards we murdered. Is it only the crimes of the rich that go unpunished? Well, quite a lot of the time, those of us who aren't so powerful get saved by a bell we call luck. Does luck exist? All these flights of thought extemporaneous to the situation somehow prevented me from pissing my pants before the terrifying barks of Mr. Bob and the exterminating cane of Fernandísimo Plaza de los Reyes. Antonieta had already done so. Was that an incriminating puddle of... water... at her feet? When Fernandísimo noticed, he fell quiet and lowered his stick. Mr. Bob suddenly stopped his barking, sniffed the puddle, and, apparently, realizing it was nothing to do with a bitch, went to sit on his master's chair. Then Fernandísimo began to roar with laughter. The expression on his face switched a hundred and eighty degrees and now portrayed a strange mixture of mockery, good humor and a touch of affection. In his eyes I seemed to perceive a flash of friendship once again.

— You peed yourself, kid! Hahaha... Very, very good! That really is authentic! It's impossible to pretend to piss!

We frowned and looked at each other.

— Your fear was as authentic as your urine on my parquet. The sad thing about all this is that you believed a lie just as you have done all your life, as you have done, Antonieta, your whole life and as I have done all my life too and anyone else you can find in any part of the world.

I don't know if I was hallucinating at that instant, but it seemed to me that Mr. Bob laughed after his last word. Is it possible for a dog to laugh? We don't know. Maybe they do. But to laugh with a human laugh? Well, I was getting to a point in my life where I realized that I knew nothing at all and that anything was possible. I think it was Socrates that said "The only thing I know is that I know nothing". I think he should've added: "But all I know is that in this world, without money you can't get anywhere." So I kept listening to the words of Fernandísimo Plaza de los Reyes to see if I could still discern a possibility of us being his heirs. That flash of friendship in his eyes had renewed my hope. I wasn't wrong, was I?

— Dear friends, how easy it is to deceive another human being! You believed my mask number fifty-five! I was acting, acting, acting, acting! I wasn't angry. I just wanted to see how you would react. Let's say I did it to see a bit of truth in you. And I saw it. That piss is behavior you can't fake and your face of anguish and disappointment, Antonieta, just the same. There are times like now when the masks slip in spite of ourselves and we show an infinitesimal glimpse of what we really feel or are. But that lasts a thousand times less than a sneeze. Then we go back to the masquerade. That's what's best for us in this orgy of hypocrisy. Why would I be angry, for God's sake! You let the cat out of the bag, but I already knew. The lie of your friendship... No, don't worry... I thank you for that lie. It's a compassionate lie and deserves a reward: my inheritance.

Antonieta and I looked at each other and breathed a sigh of relief. Fernandísimo continued.

— After all, we live a world of lies. The world we have created is a big lie... including God.

Mr. Bob seemed to utter a single bark of protest. We opened our eyes wide and then softened our expressions, performing a questioning smile. Fernandísimo extended the pause to a theatrical degree and then stated:

— I mean particularly... the idea we form of God.

After these words I seemed to hear the ringing of church bells. Was there a church around here? I felt that I was beginning to doubt myself. Or had I always doubted myself? What Fernandísimo de Reyes said to us moments later deepened my doubts about myself, about the human condition, about the canine condition, and gave Antonieta and me a new and terrifying challenge.

Chapter 21

Tarud Arab had grown thinner and his eyes were bulging out of his head ready to pop out. Some very deep and black bags under his eyes were reminiscent of a cadaver. After a flood, how many things can happen? Not just a dove with an olive branch in its beak, but also a black and heartrending bird of prey. Many months had passed, the streets had dried up, the mud had been removed with heavy machinery, the corpses had been piled up and cremated, the sobbing had fallen silent and the Municipal Theater had been rebuilt. The show must go on. And that was what Tarud Arab screamed constantly and directly into the ears of Simone Chantal. Shortly after the catastrophe, the woman had sat on a couch in front of the window from which she saw a weeping willow that didn't look green with hope but had a sad greenness. And there she remained for months, still and silent, her gaze lost beyond the weeping willow. The show must go on, you French shit! You are making me lose not just thousands, but millions of pesos! The TV station can't wait any longer. Our contract will expire. They can't go on repeating recordings of old programs any longer. You need to come back live and direct. They can't continue deceiving the public. They told me that if you don't show up on the set this week, they will hire an Armenian medium who agrees to work for less than half of what they pay us, and she has the attraction of working with Egyptian mummies that she takes to the studio so they can communicate with her from the afterlife, and the mummies often move when their voices are heard from beyond the grave. They are sure they can get hundred percent ratings with the Armenian! The only one who has insisted on waiting for you, at the risk of losing his position as general manager of the channel, is Aceituno Mendoza, who has confessed to me that he is only doing so because you drive him crazy in bed and because he doesn't like Armenians for such tasks. Did you hear me, you Parisian bitch!?

For the first time after so long, there was a glimmer of sunlight. Simone smiled and a sparkle came into her eyes. Tarud Arab preferred then to swallow back the words he was about to vomit out. Simone continued look beyond the willow tree, but now with a smile and with a very soft voice she said:

— What a discriminatory man that Aceituno Mendoza is. And prejudiced too. Why not with the Armenian?

Arab didn't dare say anything. She smiled again.

— They're puppets.

This time the cadaverous Tarud Arab dared to interject.

— Who are puppets, Simone?

She didn't reply.

— Simone, who?

And this time, after so long, Madame Chantal rose to her feet and, almost in an energetic cry, said:

— Those mummies! Those mummies are puppets!

And Tarud Arab:

— Simone, blessed be God!

— Shut up, you heretic! You have never believed in God!

And again Tarud Arab:

— But now I do! This is a miracle!

— Let's go to the TV station right now. You'll see what a miracle it is!

Tarud Arab sighed in relief. The dark circles disappeared, his eyes settled back into their orbits, and some slight color even flushed back to his face.

The woman sang Édith Piaf's repertoire while she dressed and Tarud Arab smartened himself up while singing in Arabic the "Song of the Camel that encountered a tank of General Rommel when it arrived at El Alamein." The rather long title made it seem doubtful that the song had actually been composed by someone, aside from the fact that the melody, rather than music, was more reminiscent of a cave-dwelling stoneworker. Arab always insisted that the song had been composed by one of Ali Baba's forty thieves. In response to questions like, what, did they really exist? Aren't they just characters in a story? Or how come that thief was alive during the Second World War, he answered with another question: "Have you never heard of the Count of Saint Germain?" No one continued asking. The matter was too complicated and it was better to be the one who swallowed the tale. Be that as it may, between the songs of Piaf and the tune composed by Ali Baba's fortieth thief, both were ready and they sped off to the television channel, the little goose who laid the golden eggs, whose throat they were about to cut.

Chapter 22

PRINT MEDIA

Newspaper "El Centauro":

The man with the broom, Dante Carrasco Ugarte, claims that an innumerable majority of young "real Chileans" follow him and unconditionally support his crusade to cleanse Chile of the trash into which it has been submerged by the political class and certain people of the economic elite, both united by habitual corruption. His strategy of disobeying authority is said to be working well. Chile, he stated emphatically and calmly, will cease to be the dump into which it has been converted, and with solidarity, clean hearts and sustained and unselfish commitment we will turn it into something very close to a "happy copy of Eden".

Newspaper "La Hora Última":

They are all Dante Carrasco Ugarte. A powerful businessman who prefers to remain anonymous financed the million-dollar manufacture of thousands and thousands of masks made of an expensive material with the face of the young Dante Carrasco Ugarte, the hope of a Chile worthy of true Chileans. This is why hundreds of people can be seen wearing these masks on the streets of the capital and in some of the large provincial cities in the north and south of the country. The presence of the "man with the broom" has thus multiplied exponentially. Although the financier of this significant escalation is not known, the notary public Daniel Arriagada y Pinto assured that he holds a document signed by the mysterious businessman in which he declares and undertakes never to request a political favor of any kind from Dante Carrasco Ugarte's movement should he ever come to power. The public notary said goodbye to us, but not before putting on a mask bearing Dante Carrasco's face. His final words before we left were: "As you can see, it's white. It isn't really a mask. It's more a symbol of truth, of good intentions, of goodwill and unquestionable patriotism. We are all Dante Carrasco Ugarte and Dante Carrasco Ugarte is hope and a renewed nation."

TELEVISION

Channel 55 "Ultravision":

On screen: **Putting on an angry face, the newsreader announces that thousands of masked demonstrators are taking to the streets of downtown Santiago and that their actions are undermining public order by obstructing the free transit of vehicles. To his regret and that of the press department, the cameramen shows the image of thousands of people wearing the mask representing the face of Dante Carrasco and takes close-ups of the broom that every demonstrator carries and signs stating: "DISOBEDIENCE — NO MORE CORRUPTION — FOR A DECENT CHILE FOR DECENT CHILEANS". One of the cameramen pans away and shows another cameraman with his camera on his shoulder who is already wearing the mask that is so popular and well liked by the vast majority of true Chileans. Suddenly, the broadcast turns into static and goes black. Behind the dark screen a voice says: "We apologize, we're having technical difficulties." But the technical problem is solved in seconds: The picture returns, showing a curvaceous girl in a bikini drinking a Coca-Cola. Superimposed over the attractive young woman is the legend "Coca-Cola is better than anything else".**

Channel 12 "Tele Futuro":

On screen: **Plaza Baquedano and much of Alameda Bernardo O'Higgins full of protesters wearing the white mask of Dante Carrasco Ugarte's face, sitting peacefully on the ground. They sing joyful songs and, in a calm and friendly tone, Dante Carrasco's voice calls for** *everyone to join the "disobedience" to take authority away from those who do not deserve to run the country for having turned it into a land of violence, hatred, insecurity, distrust and anguish. Suddenly, a uniformed police unit appears and begins aiming a water cannon at the protesters, who remain seated on the ground without offering resistance, stoically enduring the soaking. Abruptly, one of the policemen jumps onto one of the demonstrators, they appear to struggle a little and finally the policeman rips the mask off, exposing the face of an elderly man who protests at the action of the policeman. The policeman throws his cap into the air, puts on the mask and embraces the unmasked man, shouting: "I'm Dante Carrasco too!" Other policemen, dozens of them, advance toward the demonstrators and copy the gesture of their comrade. Caps fly skyward, the water cannon closes its valves and cheers rise up like millions of thrushes and the thousands of Chilean flags flutter freely and the wind bathes the diaphanous morning light in tricolor... ecstatic... ecstatic... ecstatic... fade out!*

RADIO

CB-114 Radio "La Verdad":

Breaking News. The Chilean Ministry of Justice and Gendarmerie reported that at 4:00 a.m. this morning Johnny Tunante will be executed: He is the criminal who provoked the reinstatement of the death penalty in Chile. According to the relevant legal reforms and Amendment 01, the perpetrator will die by lethal injection, a procedure that will be carried out in the modern facilities built for this purpose. The execution will be broadcast live on national television. Nevertheless, it will also be recorded to be rebroadcast during the daytime so that all of Chile can witness the sobering spectacle... sorry, the sobering execution. And now we continue with our cheerful dance music program. Bring on the music on CB-114 Radio La Verdad!... José y sus Negros Gozadores!... Move your ass, girl; that looks better! CUMBIA-LOVERS' MUSIC.

Chapter 23

The goose that laid the golden eggs was waiting for them with its wings spread open. The lighting grille highlighted the exotic colors of the set, the cable guys and floor managers ready in their positions, the audio controllers with attentive ears, the video controllers with their "coke bottle" glasses, the six cameras pointing precisely at different angles, the director on the switch moving his fingers like a pianist before a concert, the presenter with his toothy smile set in advance and the audience in the studio leaning forward in their seats, holding their breath in expectation.

There was no time for dressing rooms or makeup. Madame Chantal and Tarud Arab came running onto the set. The presenter raised his arms like a politician who greets the mob with a hackneyed and unspontaneous gesture:

— Here, ladies and gentlemen, viewers aaaaall over the country, is Madame Chantal, The Psychic of Paris, who, after months of absence due to having been needed in the mysterious, fascinating and ancient cultures of the Far East, returns, as always, to reveal what the future holds for us! A big round of applause for her!

But there was neither a big round applause nor even a small one. Not even a fly stirred. First there was a silence and then a loud "Aaaaaahhh!" from the public. Madame Chantal had cut the applause short when, as she came onto the set, she faced the audience, tugged at her blouse and let her huge and, by that time, somewhat droopy boobs pop out. Without giving anyone time to draw breath, she pulled her wig off, threw it at one of the cameras, and displayed her real hair, short and plastered to her head as if she were Joan of Arc about to die at the stake. "Aaaaaahhh!" To top it all off, she turned, approached the table where the production team had placed the spectacular crystal ball, grabbed it, looked at the audience and raised it aloft. She didn't let it drop, but instead launched it into the floor with the violence and power of a bomb. The ball exploded into thousands of pieces of ordinary glass that had been claimed to be fine crystal. "Oooooohhh!" By this stage, Tarud Arab already lay stretched out and stiff on the ground, either fainted or dead. The madame didn't even notice and, even if she had, she would have done exactly the same thing. The cameramen insisted on taking close-ups of her somewhat sad and tired breasts. So when Simone Chantal spoke, all the viewers at home could see were two talking tits that moved a little up and down and left to right depending on her movements and gesticulations.

— The show is over, you crowd of open-mouthed morons who have the wool pulled over your eyes right down to your feet. I am not what you have seen or what they have told you about me. This is me!

Having said that, she removed the rest of her clothes and stood naked like an egg without a scrap of shell.

— This is me! A stupid Frenchwoman who believed the stories of the communists, who came to Chile to play revolution and then became a whore, more for pleasure than out of necessity and later became even more of a whore to be a fucking TV star. Wake up, fools and idiots, I and much worse are the kind of people you adore, worship and obey. The farce is over, *merde*!

And without another word she leapt away and disappeared through one of the doors of the studio. The director on the switch had taken off his headphones because the volume of the crazy Frenchwoman's cries had almost burst his eardrums, but he said to the staff nearby: "At least we got some excellent material. What people see at home during the news will boost the rating one hundred percent. Then will come the whole campaign to smear that idiot and public opinion will remember her as a lunatic. We'll save our reputation." He went down to the set and, seeing Tarud Arab's pale and stiff body lying on the floor, he shouted over the speakers: "Someone cover that body with a sheet! Pablo, did you get a shot of the corpse?"

When the news came on, everyone saw the scandal, edited in such a way that the Frenchwoman looked like a monster possessed by a hundred demons. The images hit maximum ratings and were later sold at a very high price to both national and international television channels. Programs were filmed with forums that talked about that terrible woman and psychics and experts gave their opinions on demonic possession, others —ufologists— claimed that she could be an alien infiltrated into the world with the mission of shocking its inhabitants. The speculation grew and grew and grew, and the money grew and grew to fill the same privileged pockets as always.

Half the world was interviewed. So many people from the government, experts, opinionologists, academics, doctors, psychiatrists and others came out to speak. The only one who didn't accept any interviews, resigned his position and cloistered himself in his isolated stone house at the foot of the mountains was Guzmán Peralta. Remember him?

So many things were seen after that, but I can assure you that what no one saw was Simone Chantal, instead of jumping out of the studio door, rising into the air, naked on a flying broomstick. She gained altitude and flew over the roofs of the houses and buildings. It's true that some of the people on the streets looked up to the sky and saw her, but they didn't believe what they saw. There was an intense heat and a Coca-Cola billboard invited one to have a drink of the refreshing beverage because it was "thirst-quenching." Dying of thirst and heat and worried that they had seen a hallucination, they went to buy hundreds of Coca-Colas to cool off, satiate their thirst and eliminate the apparition from their minds and return to reality.

Simone Chantal soared far above the clouds on her broomstick and was happy. She was the eighth horseman of the Apocalypse announcing that the powers of good had triumphed.

Chapter 24

The priest arrived an hour beforehand, at exactly five p.m. Outside the brand new and modern building, a crowd led by Dante Carrasco Ugarte protested with signs that read: "They're crucifying Christ again"; "They're going to execute a sheep"; "Executioner, be part of history, disobey."

The priest sat in front of the bunk in the cell. A picture of the president hung on one of the walls. The photo had intentionally been taken out for the occasion, because in her gaze was a gleam of feigned sweetness and a smile like the Mona Lisa. At the foot of the picture of the president was written: "Son, you die by just mandate of society, but I forgive you in spirit. Go and rest in peace. The state will watch over your soul. Your mother, President."

— Do you repent, son?

— Yes, for being born in this garbage of a country.

— Fool. That wasn't your decision. It was the will of God.

— What a bad will God has for some and how good for others!

— Fool. You're about to be executed and you're blaspheming.

— Stupid priest, don't you realize that they're going to kill me and that I've done nothing?

— You idiot, you should thank them. You're going to a better life.

— How do you know it's better?

— I just know, period. It's a question of dogma. Accept it and don't ask any more questions.

— I see that this whole life has been a dogma.

— You're an idiot, but you seem educated.

— Stupid priest, I only look educated. I'm speaking by divine inspiration.

— Idiot, are you screwing with me?

— Why do you ask, excess hormones? Are you a pedophile too?

— Take back those words or I won't absolve you of your sins and you will die and go straight to hell.

—Stupid priest, you have to absolve me. That's why they're paying you.

— There's no point arguing about that, son.

— At least we agree on something. There's been a miracle.

— It seems so, son, although I don't believe in miracles.

— I do, will you believe me?

— Okay, let's hurry up as the time of your injection is approaching. Come on, make it easy for me.

— Okay.

— Wow, you know English!

— No, I only know how to say okay. That's enough. I was going to learn the rest by reading the ads for cafes and restaurants. I didn't get to learn what "happy hour", "break", "office", "retail" and so on meant... you must forgive my pronunciation. I realize that apart from me, Chileans are the English of the Americas. I've heard that from my mom since I was a kid in the cemetery.

— Okay, now let me do my job.

— Okay, Father.

— Do you repent?

— Well, alright.

— Do you believe in God the Father, Jesus Christ, the Holy Spirit and the Blessed Virgin?

— I believed in whatever I was told. That's why I'm here now.

— Do you think so?

— What do you want me to say!

— What you think.

— Well, yes.

— Alright. I absolve you. Now go and die in peace.

A bell rang. Two prison guards appeared. It's time, they said. They each grabbed Johnny Tunante by one arm and took him along the corridor. The bulbs on the ceiling flickered three times. When he reached the gate that led to the execution room, Johnny Tunante turned his head and said goodbye:

— Goodbye, stupid priest.

— Goodbye, idiot. Take care.

Two tiny tears clouded the priest's eyes a little. The gate closed with a deathly sound.

Chapter 25

Looking solemn, he made us sit in front of him. As if sensing that seriousness, Mr. Bob sat beside him on his back legs in the pose of a gargoyle.

— I have very good news for you —began Fernandísimo Plaza de los Reyes. The first thing is that I want you to know that for a long time I have taken note of your friendship towards me...

Antonieta and I looked at each other with satisfaction on hearing these words. We had convinced the old man.

— ...I have realized that your friendship towards me is completely false.

The bucket of cold water left us stiff. We would have to resign ourselves to continue living in the mediocrity of the middle class.

— The second thing is that, despite this deception, I understand you. There isn't a human being on the planet that wouldn't do anything for money in one way or another. You're young and ambitious and you want a better life than you have.

I didn't dare to start smiling with relief. Neither did Antonieta. The old man's words were always unpredictable. They took unexpected turns like an erratic spinning top.

— Therefore, thanks to my compassionate and charitable spirit, I wish to reward the great efforts that you have made as consummate actors to create that lie. I have decided to leave you as my heirs of my part of my fortune after my death.

Antonieta finally opened her mouth beset by... scruples perhaps?

— Fernandísimo... I don't know what to say... to thank you... but, first of all, to tell you that we've always liked you as a...

— Let's not continue the lies! There's no need to keep up the charade anymore! You've been unmasked, but you're my heirs!

As always Mr. Bob corroborated the words of his master. He gave a single precise bark. Plaza de los Reyes thanked him for the gesture, patting him on the head. The dog emitted a few soft grunts of pleasure. Our stern benefactor continued.

— Antonieta and Ricardo, you two will inherit one quarter of everything I own. The other three quarters of my fortune will go to my dog, Mr. Bob. He certainly deserves it. He never lies... like all of his race.

— But...

Fernandísimo raised an eyebrow, frowning, and his eye shot her a precise look:

—Any problem, Mrs. Antonieta?

— No, Don Fernandísimo, of course not.

— So... one more lie! ...but we'll let it pass.

He was silent for a few moments as if he was he pondering something and then, almost with a shout, he exploded:

— You just can't stop lying for fuck's sake! Be honest, hoooonest! Say what you feel. Say that you find it ridiculous that I'm leaving my fortune to a dog, say that you think I'm a shitty old man for preferring to give it to an animal and not to those who serve me in this house, say that you curse the one who hasn't left you two my whole fortune, say that you want me to die soon because you're dying to be rich as soon as possible! Say it, say it, say it! Show yourself as you are for once!

He shouted all this, raising his arms, waving his cane, his eyes dilated, his cheeks flushed, with his voice quavering like never before, and all this backed by the frenetic and almost uncontrolled barking of Mr. Bob, mimicking the old man's words, a thundering chorus. Antonieta just blinked like a doll on remote control and I realized we were both shits, that we were all shit and that Mr. Bob was the only one who deserved to enter the Kingdom of Heaven. Had God considered animals in his immigration policy?

It seemed that master and dog were linked by a telepathic friendship. Both fell silent at the same time, in unison in a microsecond decision. Fernandísimo Plaza de los Reyes sat back down and continued speaking, calm, serene, affable, as if he were someone else.

— Alright. Enough. My apologies. Like I said, three-quarters for Bob and a quarter for you. Don't be downhearted. That's a lot of money, a great deal of money. Consider it an Oscar for your performance. As for my employees, my workers in this house, I have already given them their share in life. Also a lot of money, so they can stop working today for the rest of their lives. But they, loyal, have told me that they will continue to work by my side as long as I need them. That is, until I become discarnate. Do you believe in reincarnation?

We both replied at the same time:

— Yes, of course... of course.

— Liars, you don't believe that! You're Catholics.

We bowed our heads. He continued.

— My employees are certainly not human. They belong to the canine race, only they don't bark. They don't have that privilege.

As we looked at him with questioning faces, he explained:

— If you can only bark it's impossible to lie. Barks aren't made for lies, nor is the song of the birds, nor the roar of the lion, nor the thunder from the heavens. But words are the vehicle of lies. "What comes out of the mouth of man defiles man," said the Lord Jesus.

We realized that our man was inspired. Was he falling into senile dementia?

— The last thing. In a few days I will finally return home.

— What do you mean, Fernandísimo? Aren't you at home now?

Antonieta's question confirmed my theory that the old man was already in full dementia.

— My friend, New York is my home.

— Have you been there before?

— Never. But my heart feels that I have. That's my original home. I've felt it since I was very young, although I only know the Big Apple through movies and photos and what my father told me about it. He often traveled for business and he worshipped that city. So I'm going back to my home. Let's see if it was in a previous incarnation!

He paused.

— Don't worry, the will is made and I'll leave you my address so they know where to find me in New York. This meeting is over. Thank you. God be with you and be happy. You have money ensured for many years of your lives. Have a nice weekend.

Once out on the street, Antonieta ran rather than walked. I followed behind her, trying to catch her so she could hear me.

— What do you think about all this?

Short of breath she replied.

— What do you want me to say! What we'll get is miserable compared to that fucking dog.

— It's something.

— Conformist just like all Chileans! We have to do something.

— Do what!

— First kill the dog and then kill the old man. Or kill them both at the same time.

— But he's going to New York.

I began to gasp too.

— We'll have to go there. It'll be easier to kill him.

— We can talk to one of the mafias. Italian, Russian, Japanese, Chinese. The one that charges least.

— And how are we going to pay them?

— Once we receive the inheritance.

— No, Antonieta, they won't accept that. They'll ask for payment in advance. At least a part.

— You have a credit card, right?

I didn't answer. I no longer had sufficient breath to speak and I was too far behind. She ran like an ostrich. I just thought: "Animals kill to survive, men to profit." A blast from a horn and screech of brakes brought me back to my senses. A truck almost crushed my wife. Unfortunately, the driver was too skilful and managed to avoid tragedy. A pity, I would have saved myself the trouble of killing Antonieta when the time came. Her guardian devil seemed to be a very alert creature.

Chapter 26

The show must go on, so the audience room was already crowded with people, press, judicial authorities, representatives of the armed forces and uniformed and plain clothes police, the Minister of the Interior and a long list of accomplices. The warden acted as host. On the other side of the glass was the white gurney, still unused, with its straps and the thin plastic tubes that would channel death into the veins and heart of Johnny Tunante. Higher up, on a sort of altar, was the executioner's glass cage for the chemist in charge of injecting somniferous drugs and then the lethal substance. Alfredo Mortimer Camposanto, Ph.D. in Applied Chemistry, Harvard University, would not only carry out the process, but had also created the relevant formula of chemicals. When he entered his cubicle, many of those present gave an exclamation of surprise and awe. The only real difference between the face of Dr. Frankenstein's monster and that of Dr. Mortimer was that the latter didn't have two bolts through his temples.

Then a quite stupendous woman with a disconcertingly curvaceous body and the face of a Hollywood star entered the execution room, dressed as a nurse. She checked the installations before giving those watching on the other side of the glass a flirtatious TV smile. Right away Johnny Tunante came in with two more beauties, also dressed as nurses. With feminine and even maternal delicacy they helped him lie down on the gurney, adjusted the straps and connected the conductive tubes. The woman who came in first asked the condemned man in the sweetest and most tender voice: "Johnny, do you want to say something before embarking on your journey?" Johnny hesitated for a few seconds and then said, "Hey, the people on the other side, the observers over there, better get me a round-trip ticket," and then he fell silent. Someone in the audience said to the person beside him: "The boy believes in reincarnation; he's not as simple as we thought". The stupendous woman who had been left alone with Johnny asked with honeyed words: "Anything else to say, Johnny?" The condemned man did not respond. Then she bent over him and offered him a tender kiss on the lips. This did elicit a response from the "murderous monster", as he had been branded by the "friends" in the press, as he tried in vain to sit up, pouting his mouth like an elephant's trunk to see if could prolong the kiss. But the woman had already stood up and was heading for the exit. Before leaving, she looked back at the audience for the last time and said: "I recommend Valerian Standardized from Gold Laboratories, the best thing to calm the nerves."

Her English was perfect, though it was the only thing she knew how to say. The truth is that in the audience room there were at least two banners advertising the product. Outside, at the entrance of the penitentiary building various other pretty promoters had been there since early, handing out free packets of Valerian capsules and giving anyone who wanted one a small cup of caffeine-free Coca-Cola (there was another billboard advertising that) so they could take them and watch the execution without any stress or discomfort. This time, the authorities' management had been impeccable.

In the observation room, a violinist and friend to the head of the Fondart Fund for Arts and Culture, who had made the winning proposal to that institution for a juicy sum to make a presentation and others in the future, began to play the mournful "Goodbye Song". Some people shed tears. After all, it was something that was looked upon with approval. While the sad melody floated through the room, an old and modest woman entered the room. Confused and frightened she stood staring, not knowing what to do. Someone saw her and said under his breath, "Sit down here, madam." She replied, "Thank you," with her mouth showing just a few sparse teeth and she sat, hands crossed on top of her skirt and her shoulders hunched. She stared at the man who was strapped to the gurney. She was Johnny Tunante's mother.

Chapter 27

It is fair and necessary to say what there is and what happens in Brooklyn, specifically in Williamsburg, very close to Bedford Street. The most amazing things, silent and almost in the anonymity of the shadows, take place in unsuspected and habitual places which, for that very reason, don't attract much attention. In this case, the building that was the first Savings Bank, built in Brooklyn in 1865, which, despite its beauty and majesty, has been there so long that it doesn't draw much attention. That said, people (or those who look at things) do look at the magnificence of its high dome, crowned with the figure of a golden being who seems to be leaping towards the sky, as well as the brilliance and beauty of its old metal, which seems relatively new thanks to the skill and talent of some anonymous artist, in the nobility of its old and gleaming woodwork, thanks again to the care of these same hands, and the imposing severe and yet gentle immobility with which it has survived the years. Some people think they know about that special building. They are convinced that it is in the hands of Argentine investors and businessmen who, with a vocation for beauty and a commercial vision, are responsible for keeping it in optimal condition, taking care to preserve every millimeter of the history and antiquity of the colossal construction. They also claim that the craftsman who makes the restoration, antiquity and art possible is a quirky artist of medium height with very long hair, blond as straw, that reaches his waist, with impressive tattoos on his arms and chest, who wears an elegant black hat adorned with a red feather on the side as if to announce his longings for freedom and flight and his detachment from the mundane, and who moves around the streets of Brooklyn and Manhattan on a colorful red bicycle. Some think they know that he was born in Chile and those people call him Chile. "Hey, Chile, come and look at these locks that have to be restored"; "Hey, Chile, you've got a beautiful hat". However, there are those who claim, without a moment's hesitation, that the guy in question is called Lucho or Luis. Well, in this case it doesn't matter. The truth is that the world in which all these people live is a simple illusion. What they see are just ghosts. Behind all of this is the truth.

The truth of the Williamsburg mansion is that Mary Mayflower, The Powerful lives inside. None of them knows that, none of them have even seen her. But that's how things really are.

The interior of that majestic architecture is enormous, stately, typical of the marbles in the palaces of the Roman empire. Counting the five underground floors and the huge central dome that rises dozens of yards up into the sky, it can be considered a building more than fifteen floors tall. At the top of the marble dome, stained glass, bronzes and steel fly seven beautiful eagles. They never descend to the brilliant ceramic floor. They are always flying in a circle or conducting beautiful aerial, attentive, watchful maneuvers. When one of them needs a rest they go and perch on the shoulders of Mary Mayflower, The Powerful. The woman is tall, blond with intensely blue eyes, a noble profile with a straight and fine nose, her age indefinable from an earthly viewpoint and her existence looks eternal. If someone passing by the building has the chance of seeing her, they would have the amazing impression that she is a young and beautiful woman, but of many years of age. She is The Powerful, as she knows and decides. Her power is almost invisible, but many times its consequences are visible. When the Enola Gay dropped its atomic bombs on Hiroshima and Nagasaki, achieving the final surrender of Japan during World War II, everyone believed that the decision and the operation came from President Truman and his military advisors. Once again the phantasmagoria of earthly reality made them all believe something different to the truth.

Since not everything can be revealed for reasons that I cannot tell, I will not say either why nor how Mary Mayflower knew that Fernandísimo Plaza de Reyes had traveled to the United States of America, and specifically to New York, with the intention of establishing himself there for the rest of his life because he somehow felt that he was returning home, even though he had never visited those iconic places before. She also knew that the man was from Chile, such a southern South American country, so South American.

When Mary Mayflower, The Powerful, uttered the name of Fernandísimo Plaza de los Reyes, lifting her arms aloft in a gesture of witchcraft and raising her voice to the top of the huge dome, announcing his imminent journey to New York, the seven eagles became agitated, flying swiftly and violently in a dance of war, emitting not the sounds of birds but unintelligible words whose sounds would have suggested dark meanings to the man in the street. And while this was happening, the seven thresholds having been crossed, many passersby walked along Broadway through Williamsburg in Brooklyn in front of the iconic nineteenth century building, stopping engrossed to watch an eccentric blond artist with hair down to his waist who was at the top of a scaffold crane at the summit of the dome, shouting to him: "Chile, don't fall", while he was busy using the secret patinas of his craft to cover the golden figure leaping towards the sky. They also paused at the cheerful, laughter-punctuated chatter that rose into the air with a Buenos Aires lilt from the Argentine businessmen at the main door of the building, while in the central hall under the Romanesque dome, Jensen, the chief carpenter, built a Bethlehem tableau for a big Christmas event with his noble and ancient craft. The festivities were about to begin.

Chapter 28

The old woman didn't take her eyes off her son, lying on his deathbed. He lay still with his eyes closed and the rhythm of his breathing was covered by the whitest of sheets. After a few moments, while the violin music continued saddening the atmosphere, the mother, keeper of tombs and mausoleums, leaned toward the person next to her and whispered in his ear: "Sir, have I arrived late? Is he already dead? The man replied, "No, you're here in time. They still haven't killed that scumbag." The old lady didn't dare say anything, but she shivered from head to toe. The man wanted to continue the conversation: "With all due respect, who are you? The mother of one of the victims? "This time the woman did dare to reply, "No, sir, I'm the mother of the only victim. I am the mother of the boy on the other side of the glass." The man felt all his blood drain down to his feet and he went paler than the corpse that would be put on display. He hurriedly got up and went to sit at the back of the room. When he realized he was the only one in that row of seats, he felt a fit of laughter and had to stifle it by covering his mouth with both hands and turning so red that anyone seeing him would have thought he was about to burst. To make matters worse, the violinist stopped playing and a deathly silence settled on the room. The execution was seconds away from starting and justice just instants from raising her sword in her double role as executioner and goddess of equity and rectitude.

When the Harvard Doctor of Chemistry, Alfredo Mortimer Camposanto, raised his thumb to signal that he was ready to proceed and the warden on the other side winked in respect for diversity, Johnny Tunante's last few moments began to come to an end. The Chilean Frankenstein's monster pressed the plunger of the first injector. A sky blue liquid could be seen moving through the tubes and entering the veins of that jackal. He breathed as if sighing with relief and then it was clear that he had fallen fast asleep. The hands of the little old woman began to shake. The others were enjoying the procedure. There were three injections. Two left. The warden again closed one eye, this time with greater sympathy. The Harvard Doctor of Chemistry ignored the gesture, but obeyed the order, or was it a suggestion? He squeezed the second plunger. A green mixture crept into the martyr's body like an eager snake. Johnny Tunante shuddered with a violent convulsion of his whole body, opened his jaw and then snapped it shut, closing his lips like an air-tight box. Had she been on that side of the room, his mother would have heard a grinding of teeth. Then he was immobile. The poor old lady could contain herself no longer. She let out a long, heart-piercing sob like the howl of a wounded wolf. Then a voice from the back rose imperiously: "Ma'am, avoid expressions of hysteria. This is neither the time nor the place. You should probably leave if you can't contain yourself and take a Valerian capsule. Once you're calm you can come back if you don't want to miss the end. But Johnny Tunante's mother ignored it. However, she suppressed the expression of her pain and remained silent with her head bowed.

The final moment had come. It was time to inject the last and lethal liquid. This time, the warden was affected. He knew that this last injection would mean certain death for that poor fellow human, whose unjust conviction he was, of course, not unaware of. He had scruples, and this time he didn't wink. He nodded his head solemnly. Frankenstein's monster, the Doctor of Chemistry from Harvard University, placed his hand on the final plunger and, before pressing it, a strange smile came to his lips. Was he unable to conceal the satisfaction of knowing that he was the executioner and would go down in history? He injected death with unusual speed into the veins of the jackal. It was a black, viscous liquid. Johnny Tunante shook, made some death rattles and the immobility of death finally turned his body into a thing. Everyone looked on avidly. His body now had the somber classification of being a corpse. His mother's lips tightened. With all her might she clutched her belly with those small, wrinkled hands, stained with the freckles of age. She made a desperate effort to hold in a mortal hemorrhage of sobs. The authority of a voice at the back of the room had even been capable of suppressing her natural instincts. State authority was on its way to controlling even one's breath.

Politicians' pleasure is to feel like gods, but gods of the underworld. After a silence that at first seemed to be a gesture of reverence, the audience began to applaud. Frankenstein's monster on the other side responded by bowing like a stripper at the end of a show. The violinist contracted by Fondart then resumed his music, playing Beethoven's Funeral March. The applause continued as if requesting an encore. It was impossible. There would have had to be a second convict awaiting his turn on death row, assisted by the stunning blonde in charge of preparing him. But, for the moment there was no second condemned man. More would come. It's always good to have some guilty party and a scapegoat. So it is that the pack of miscreants that handle the herd will always appear to be the good and righteous.

Surrounded by applause, the old woman remained in her seat bent forward as if she wanted to curl into a ball and in silence she wept, concealing her convulsive sobs. The doctor in charge of verifying and certifying the convict's death entered the execution room. He leaned over the corpse with his stethoscope to listen to the stillness of death. That was when he suddenly jumped back, terrified. It was a burst of laughter. An explosion, a laugh that was expelled with the force of a geyser and which continued, growing and growing into a crescendo of uncontained laughter without stopping for a second. The applause halted like a sudden blackout and the violinist was silenced as if shot by a sniper. It was the dead man. The dead man had woken up dying of laughter.

Chapter 29

— Antonieta, he called me.

— Who?

— Fernandísimo.

— What did he say? Has he abandoned the idea of giving almost all his inheritance to the dog?

— No, he wants us to go and say goodbye.

— What! He's leaving already?

— Yeah, he's finally going to New York. "I'm going home," he told me. He sounded delighted. He insists that New York is his home despite having never set foot in the city.

— What time does his flight leave?

— In an hour. We have to hurry.

— Which flight is he on? Which airline?

— None of them. He told me that in the end he decided to rent a private plane for himself; for him and Mr. Bob. Get dressed and let's go. Ah!... it's not a good idea to sunbathe naked out here on the balcony. Look around, there's a considerable number of people watching you with telescopes from the other buildings. Look at that guy filming you.

— That's what I want, to be famous somehow. I bet more than one of them uploads me to the internet. Imagine the amount of downloads later.

— But for free. Don't be a cheap whore, honey.

— I'm not doing it for the money. I'm doing it for the fame. Money doesn't worry me now. We'll soon be rich when we kill the dog and his master. Wouldn't it be possible to speak to a mechanic at the airport and see if we can persuade him to loosen some piece of the engine so that the airplane fails in mid-flight?

— Not a bad idea, but difficult at this stage. We're too close to his departure. We don't know anyone. In any case, don't take long. *Noblesse oblige.* We have to be there to say goodbye.

She paid heed to me. Antonieta didn't even take ten minutes to get dressed. She put on a very short red miniskirt, an olive-green military parka with a sergeant's insignia on the left sleeve, which reached down to a few centimeters below her knee, a military cap and sunglasses like the ones that air force pilots wore. Her feet were shod in uniform style too, with medium-sized sneakers made of a fabric with green-brown military camouflage.

— I have to give him a sendoff with military honors. And this is also my combat outfit for when we go to New York to kill him. Our military operation begins today. You should be thinking of an outfit like this too. This operation, "death to the dog", requires a military mentality, cool, collected, tactical and prescient. You begin to be military just by putting the uniform on. The clothes make the doll —Antonieta said with cheerful, youthful and hysterical laughter.

I replied:

— It isn't just the military who are cool and calculating when they kill. It's enough just not to be a dog.

And we left for the airport.

Chapter 30

The warden shouted furiously:

— Doctor Mortimer, what blunder have you made?!

Mortimer replied from his booth using the microphone:

— It looks like my formula failed. Something must have happened in my head.

The warden:

— Idiot. What's going to happen now is that you'll be left without a head. We'll have to reform the Constitution and consider the guillotine to cut it off.

People screamed in shock. A few of them laughed along with the gleeful corpse. Happiest of all was the old lady, who now jumped for joy like a little monkey and cried, clapping her hands:

— Blessed be God! My boy, you beat these executioners and murderers! Just keep laughing, my little boy. Laugh at them!

Johnny Tunante's laughter was increasing, dangerously quickly. He was straining to free himself from the straps that held him tight. It was clear that his laughter was choking him.

— Do something —the warden said. The law must be fulfilled. Let the gendarme go in and finish him off with a bullet.

The typical voice of a woman involved in politics rose up instantly:

— That can't be done. I'm the Chair of the Commission on Human Rights. No bullets. That's violence.

The warden was beside himself:

— Stick your human rights up your ass, you fucking communist! Shoot that filthy die-hard criminal!

But the laughter had already reached its peak and in that millionth of a second, Johnny Tunante died suddenly and definitively. The bullet wouldn't have been needed, had someone complied with the order. Johnny had died from his own laughter. The old lady stood still, perplexed. The doctor approached the corpse again very gingerly. He listened. He waited a few seconds. Nothing, just a black silence in the body. Then he raised both arms in triumph and yelled in elation:

— Now he really is dead, and for good!

There was a "hurray!" in unison in the audience room and the violinist, dancing like a leprechaun on a tin roof began to play the merry song "Oh! Susanna. Now don't you cry for me." Everyone was happy and content. The law had been fulfilled, justice had been done. The warden called the Chilean Frankenstein's monster in a conciliatory tone:

— Come on, doctor, let's shake hands. Forgive my outburst a moment ago. You're a genius. Killing a man with laughter. What a great headline, what an increase in the popularity of our government. The government and the Chilean state, a happy example to the world, give the formula to condemn extreme delinquents to a happy death. In Chile, the law executes its convicts, killing them of laughter. Now joy has finally arrived in Chile.

Dr. Mortimer Camposanto, Ph.D. in Chemistry from Harvard University, the Chilean Frankenstein's monster, smiled a condescending smile. But then he stared into space and was lost from his surroundings. He thought: "I failed, the dose was excessive; I hope they don't find the white mask of Dante Carrasco Ugarte hidden in the basement of my lab."

The old woman, the tomb-keeper, walked in front of him. She was sad again, but resigned. Curiously she looked into his eyes with an inexplicable hint of friendship and gratitude. He answered that look with a smile that sweetened his monstrous face. She also responded with a smile and continued toward the exit. The tender Frankenstein watched her she walked away. Mothers have an unerring instinct.

Chapter 31

We arrived on time. We were able to get onto the tarmac of the airport after a few discussions and some Kafkaesque bureaucracy. The private plane leased by Fernandísimo was a beautiful one of an excellent breed. It looked like an upper-class bird, long, tapering and slender, with wings that seemed like fine fins that stretched toward the tail, which pointed high to the sky. The four turbines, two under each wing, looked like instruments of speed, both discreet and elegant. It was an intensely red Italian bird that would surely make plenty of passersby look up when it flew over Manhattan. It was a bird ready to conquer New York. That was how Fernandísimo Plaza de los Reyes must have felt when he was ready to climb the stairway of the aircraft, preceded by Mr. Bob. The eyes of both, master and animal, shone with hope.

— I thought you weren't coming. Bob and I were a little disappointed.

— Sorry, Fernandísimo. You know, the hassles at airports.

— Or the habit of leaving everything to the last minute, my friend. But, in the end, now you're here. I needed to see my heirs come to say goodbye at least. For your peace of mind, everything has been settled and the papers are signed and in the hands of the executor and lawyer.

— We didn't just come to say goodbye. We promise to come and visit you in New York too. You'll have a little place for us to stay, won't you Fernandísimo? —said Antonieta with a smile. Though was it macabre or pleasant?

I've learned not to be sure of what I perceive. I don't know if what I see is what I see or if what I think is what I think or if I think it is because I want to think it is or because someone make me think that way or because I can't think otherwise. So many things experienced and so many projects for the future, some certainly not entirely innocent. They've made me a fetus. At that moment I tried to look at Plaza de los Reyes not as my future victim but as my benefactor and friend. The same for the animal. Mr. Bob had given me a kindly look and then deep within me I wanted to be a man who loved animals. I looked at Antonieta. I knew that she be would be my victim too. But something made me sad. I regretted not being a good human being and felt that the only victim there was myself. I was my own antagonist. How could I avoid that, God?

— My dear Antonieta. I'm going back home. New York is my home, my place on the planet and, therefore, New York will be the place where you'll be able to stay.

Fernandísimo's voice sounded content, convinced, full of positive feelings, good wishes, charged with happiness.

— Thank you, my friend, thank you. What I don't understand is how you can feel like that when you've never been to New York before.

Antonieta had expressed herself sincerely. A drop of truth at last.

— That's right, Antonieta. But you never know. Maybe I was there once before. Many are the dwellings of my Father, says Jesus. In any case, the mysteries of life.

He said this smiling benevolently and condescendingly. Antonieta stiffened.

— Anyway, did you see what happened to the French fortuneteller, that Madame… Chantal? It was all a fraud that she herself confessed in the middle of a live TV program.

— Yes, that's right, and the guy who represented her, Tarud Arab, the main agent of the lie, died of a heart attack right there.

Fernandísimo was objective and calm when he said those words.

— But I imagine you won't continue believing in those mental powers that the French witch made you believe you had —insisted Antonieta somewhat scathingly.

— Why not?

— But…

— Listen to me, my friend. We live in a world where everything is a lie and we believe in those lies and we move because of those lies. The only thing is that they aren't admitted lies. That woman's lie because a more honest one, because she confessed to it. I know she lied to me, but that lie left a fragrance in my soul that it's good not to lose. I'll feel safer over there believing that I have the power to do something good for that country that

I love so much. Didn't you feel sad and stop being the young girl you once were when you discovered that Santa Claus didn't exist? That's a lie that should never be admitted because it's a good lie, an affectionate fantasy of the soul, a remote longing for love that man has deep within.

When I heard Fernandísimo speak like that, I felt like even more of a scumbag. The impetus and the neurosis of being his killer vanished. But a huge hundred-dollar bill that ran through me from temple to temple gave me a shake me and reminded me that sentimentality and good deeds don't produce much money and that in this life it's money that rules. The engines began to whine. Mr. Bob, who seemed to know all along, climbed the stairway and entered the plane. Fernandísimo hugged us, climbed up and before disappearing through the door he raised both arms like an international leader, like a person destined to appear in bronze, marble and history very soon.

The plane started taxiing to the end of the runway. The powerful blast of the turbines blew both my hat and Antonieta's cap far away. Even so, she saluted, raising her hand in military fashion to her right temple and clicking her heels together. Fernandísimo departed in the appropriate manner and with the obligatory military honors. Within a couple of minutes we watched as the plane, a blazing firebird, took off into starry blue skies that would take him to the Apple of the World.

Chapter 32

T he red bird had already risen above the highest clouds and flew in open, clear, limpid and infinite skies. Mr. Bob looked out of the window with the civilized attitude of a dog of class. Fernandísimo Plaza de los Reyes lounged on one of the comfortable leather sofas behind a glass table, savoring short and slow sips of one of those whiskeys reserved only for the wealthiest people on the planet. The cabin chief and her two assistants, three young women, one blonde, one brunette and the other black, attentively awaited any request from the only passenger on the plane. Each of them was a Miss Universe beauty in her own race. All three were the combination and essence of universal feminine loveliness. Femininity, delicacy, grace, elegance, charm and subtle, but express invitation to lust. It was a shame for Fernandísimo that he could no longer lay claim to such pleasures, given his advanced age and his health, so lust was far from his thoughts as soon as my enemy brushed his face with his tail. The fellow was doing well. He was happy, excited, full of hope. He was going to be reborn in the land he loved, in the country in which he would have chosen to be born had he been given the choice. Because of certain variables that cannot be changed, it's interesting to observe what men do with their free will framed within those parameters. Sometimes they try to change conditions and statuses that I have imposed upon them and they resort to artifices of the world that they have constructed, but deep down and in spite of appearances, that condition or status persists. I won't explain why. Sometimes it's good for man to think, although he does it very rarely. They're convinced that they think every day, that they are highly rational, but that's just an illusion.

The faint and pleasant sound of a gong resonated. The cabin chief headed to the cockpit, but not before aiming a smile at Fernandísimo. She opened the door and quickly closed it behind her. Fernandísimo glimpsed something in the millisecond during which a sliver of the interior was visible between the door rapidly opening and closing. He wasn't sure if he had seen something and if so he didn't know exactly what. But, without knowing why, it worried him. He had the impression of having seen something threatening or something that perhaps he interpreted as a threat. The uneasiness made his intestines feel uncomfortable. His colonic cancer? His altered parasympathetic nervous system? Fear? Anxiety? Adrenaline ready to act in desperate defense? What was it? Why did he start thinking about fanatical Muslims? About Al Qaeda and things like that? Mr. Bob, in tune with his master, also felt uneasy. He barked twice and then turned on the seat, returning to his starting position, but now looking fixedly at his master, seeking some response. There was the steady, subdued and continuous sound of the engines out there in the open sky. Fernandísimo smiled at his dog and stroked his head, but at the same time he swallowed hard. Suddenly, the plane shook violently. Fernandísimo turned pale, taking on something of the appearance of a corpse. Mr. Bob howled like a wolf on the steppe. The black stewardess smiled at them. Her voice was soft, feminine like velvet with a clear, sure, cultured accent: "There's no problem. It's just turbulence. This is an area of turbulence, but we'll pass through it in less than three minutes." She definitely knew something about navigation. Another shake. Oh, my God! Plenty of people only think of me when they're scared. But there are certain things that I have written and that I simply can't change. That is, I could change them if I wanted to, but I respect myself. It's only those creatures who aren't faithful to themselves.

The door of the cabin opened forcefully and the cabin chief appeared, slamming the door shut once more with equal violence. Fernandísimo was on guard, his whole body tense and he asked with his heart in his mouth:

— Is something wrong? A navigational failure? Are we going down?

Another jolt. Mr. Bob ended up on the floor and barked in annoyance.

— Not for the moment —said the cabin chief— Perhaps later?

— What do you mean? Fernandísimo's voice was pleading.

Madame Chantal had not predicted that he would die in an aviation accident. After all, and despite her scandalous confession on television, she must have had some powers of divination. She had been where she was for some reason, and perhaps she herself had never suspected she truly had the power of clairvoyance. He was sure that in the end, he, Fernandísimo Plaza de los Reyes, was going to tell the Americans where Osama Bin Laden was hiding and would become the new Superman of the States. Clinging onto our own lies sometimes helps in times of threat and horror. Another shudder, this time with the plane dropping about two hundred meters. Now Fernandísimo not only had his heart in his mouth, but his stomach and intestines too.

— The captain wants and invites you to go to the cockpit. He wishes to talk to you.

— How serious is the situation? Will my heirs be millionaires so soon?

She opened the door and merely said:

— Go in.

As soon as he entered the cockpit, Fernandísimo froze. He saw the pilot, the copilot and the flight engineer. The flight engineer sitting behind the other two was a dark-skinned man with a thick black beard and Arabic features. From behind the copilot looked like a young blond man wearing an aviator's cap. The pilot, sitting to the right, wore a huge turban. Now he thought he remembered what he had seen that troubled him. It appeared his suspicions were correct.

The pilot, the man in the turban, turned to him with a smile.

— Don't you remember me?

— You!

— Yes me. Tarud Arab.

— But you were dead.

— I was resurrected. What do you think about that?

And he smiled, more alive and kicking than ever.

Chapter 33

The tall, athletic man, dressed in gray and wearing dark glasses, had been waiting for almost two hours on one of the corners where the streets San Diego and Tarapacá meet in Santiago. He walked quietly and calmly along San Diego. Then he walked down Tarapacá. Returning to the corner, he sat for long minutes on a bench that was there at the time. He followed that routine with the precision of a stopwatch. Repeatedly, although at long intervals, a black car with tinted glass drove past the man. The occupants seemed to be watching him. The man in the dark glasses gave the impression that he was unaware of it. One of the times when he was sitting down, a modest old lady passed by him, holding the hand of a pretty little girl, no more than five years old or thereabouts. She shot him a startled sideways look. The dark lenses had intimidated her so the man smiled at her.

— Hello, little girl. Come on, don't be scared... Lady, just a moment please.

The old lady stopped.

— Yes, mister?

The guy didn't answer immediately. He had stopped smiling and, very slowly, he slipped his hand into one of his pockets. He looked at them both from behind the darkness of his glasses.

— Yes mister?

The unassuming lady was starting to get nervous. The little girl was still scared.

Suddenly the man took his hand out of his pocket.

Both the woman and the girl uttered an exclamation of surprise. Were they grateful? Intimidated? Frightened?

He held out his hand and showed them a wad of bills.

The old lady recovered a little and was able to ask:

— Do you want us to buy you something, sir?"

The little girl looked up at her... grandmother perhaps? The man replied:

— No, please. This is for you. I hope you're not offended. But you don't seem to be in a very good state. Accept this money, ma'am. At least it'll mean that today has been productive and I'll be able to fulfill what God tells us to do.

The lady mumbled a few words to refuse the gift.

— Ma'am, please accept it. What is written is written. This is meant for you.

The old lady accepted and left. She forgot to say thanks, thought the man.

The black car with the tinted windows passed in front of him again and, behind his dark glasses, he didn't seem to notice anything. Looking at them from here, men are quite laughable. They don't realize that they are a caricature just like the ones they often draw in their comics. They take everything they have invented and built far too seriously. What a way to be slaves of themselves, and after having created them to be free too.

Suddenly there was the sound of violent braking and a scream of horror. The man didn't move from the bench on which he sat, but he looked in the direction of the incident. More than half a block up the street, a truck had halted in the middle of the road. Not only was it obstructing the traffic, but beneath its front wheels lay the old woman and the little girl. Were they dead?

— The truck's killed them — shouted a woman.

The man didn't raise an eyebrow. He continued sitting. Should he go and get his money back? They weren't going to need it anymore. But he remained seated. He decided not to.

Then came the procedures and protocols. The police, the prosecutor, the legal medical team, the ambulance, the uniformed police's Department of Traffic Accidents and the inevitable press, ready to disfigure the facts and transform them into a lie called news, a profitable product of the industry of deception, bias and brainwashing.

When all this had ended, the bodies were collected, the truck taken away and the curious onlookers dissipated, the police closed Tarapacá street from that point toward the east so lots of blocks in that direction were clear, free from all traffic.

At no time did the man move from his seat. When one of the onlookers passed in front of him, he asked:

— Did you hear about what happened to the person who got run over? The passerby replied:

— It was horrible. It was an old woman and a little girl. Both dead.

— Oh my God! Exclaimed the seated man. May God take them with him.

— Let's hope so —answered the passerby and went on his way.

When he was alone, the guy with the sunglasses smiled slightly. He continued waiting. Suddenly, the black car reappeared, but at speed, and someone from within threw out an empty beer can. It rolled over to the feet of the long waiting fellow, who stood up on alert.

They were coming. There were three masked men. All three with their faces covered, wearing the white mask with the face of Dante Carrasco Ugarte. All three of almost exact the same stature, all three wearing blue jeans, all three in white sneakers, all three walking energetically at the same pace like a military unit.

The man let them pass by a good distance. They went down Tarapacá street to the east. He followed behind them. One of the Dante Carrascos turned as he felt the presence of someone following. When he saw him, the man with the dark glasses raised his thumb as if to say, "OK, I'm with you, I'm a Dante Carrasco too." The man who had turned replied with the same gesture and moved on at the pace of the other two. The street was clear. Not even a car passed. The police had blocked the traffic. Were they police? Suddenly, the man in the dark glasses pulled out a .45 automatic pistol and fired. One, two, three, four shots in a row. The impacts sounded dry, harsh and alarming. There were shouts from passersby. Some of them threw themselves to the ground like they had seen in the movies. Two of the Dante Carrascos dropped and then, with the speed of champion athletes, they got up and ran off, one turning towards Serrano street and the other straight up Tarapacá. At the next corner he turned left towards Alameda Bernardo O'Higgins. The third Dante Carrasco, who was between the other two, lay on the sidewalk lying face down in a pool of blood. Two impacts in the back of his neck and two in the back had shattered his spine.

The black car abruptly appeared. Someone opened the back door and the man in black with the sunglasses jumped inside before it had come to a halt. The door slammed shut and the car sped off, tires squealing down Tarapacá, heading east, completely free of all obstructions.

The first curious onlookers, who had had the fright of their lives, formed a circle around the body. Exclamations, sighs, stupid comments, theories about the events. "A terrorist attack; they were Al Qaeda; no, other more extreme ones; they were Zionist Jews; don't be stupid, this is the work of the Communists; I think it was a group of pedophile priests; wasn't it those from the national football team? No, I say it was the CIA; what CIA? That was your fucking communist KGB; what're you talking about, that was Mossad; I think it was the fascists like always. Well, maybe them and the Nazis and, what do you think, maybe it was a crime of passion? Did you see the guy who jumped into the black car and got away in it? I saw him waiting on that bench, going backwards and forwards for more than an hour and he showed every sign of being gay."

The police arrived, cleared away the gawkers, and then all the usual procedures, the bureaucracy of the police, the state, the judiciary, the press again. And then the prosecutor arrived. He turned over the corpse with the help of the Legal Medical Service staff. They took off his mask.

The dead man was Dante Carrasco Ugarte himself.

More than one person said they that they'd thought they'd seen the old woman and the little girl who had been run over earlier, watching on from a distance from a corner, half-hidden behind a post, looking at the corpse of the leader of the civil disobedience movement.

Chapter 34

Cause and effect. You have to be very careful about what you do because what it always has consequences. Sometimes these consequences are predictable, but other times they aren't. The murder of Dante Carrasco Ugarte brought consequences that were never expected by those who plotted the crime. Man is never saved from himself because he lives bound to himself, worshipping himself.

Dante Carrasco Ugarte wasn't considered to be a victim because those who followed him, who were the majority, refused to consider him such. Nor did they demand "justice," that is, to locate the culprits in order to hang them from their testicles and enjoy their slow agony, because they understood that that wouldn't be justice but revenge, and that with nobody wins with revenge. Chile was beginning to take a step forward and was preparing to emerge from the darkness.

What began to happen as a result of the error by his assassins was something that could not have pleased me more. Three quarters of the country covered their faces with the white masks representing Dante Carrasco. In streets, offices, police stations, warships, regiments, air bases, supermarkets, banks, brothels, squares, parks, churches, the offices of political parties and in hundreds of other places, people wore the white mask of cleanliness and hope. That's when the disobedience began. Those who refused to wear the mask and had some kind of power insisted on ordering people to remove it. But the orders from the General, the Admiral, the General Manager, the Boss, the Foreman, the powerful Politician, the dogmatic Professor, the Bishop, the Madam of the brothel, the Priest and the Guru merely echoed in the void. Everyone continued wearing their masks and even sleeping with them on. Then the General became a general, the Admiral an admiral, the General Manager a general manager, the Boss a boss, the Foreman a foreman, the Politician a politician, the Bishop a bishop, the Madam a madam, the Priest a priest, and the Guru a guru. They gritted their teeth, bit their nails, got irritable colons, but nobody, nobody obeyed them. And when no one else obeyed their other orders, the baseless, twisted, arrogant and arbitrary orders they used to impose became nothing. The country was left in the hands of a multitude of masked people ready to obey me, so they sensed that things were going well. The pollution began to disappear in Santiago and the air became fresh, healthy, transparent. Peace began to flood into people's hearts. Already the conceited, vain, arrogant, stupid, ignorant, pretentious, self-satisfied, narcissists, charlatans and liars, the corrupt and the thieves and potential murderers had seen their power vanish. The very people who had granted them that power woke up and took it away from them. "You have power over me because I fear you and because of that I obey you. But I know that there is Someone else above you and above me and so I stopped being afraid of you and I stopped obeying you and I know that I have Someone to protect me from all evil, amen."

So, from one day to the next, as simply as the sun rises in the east, everything began to change for the better. Those without masks began to abandon their fortresses, bunkers and burrows. They left the National Congress building like frightened mice and taking only what they were wearing. From the Moneda presidential palace they came out skulking with their tails between their legs and without honors or fanfare; from the barracks the generals came out without epaulettes or insignias, without the sound of a bugle, without pennants. Those without masks came out from everywhere without red carpets and in the most absolute solitude. Nobody hurt them, no one tried to harm them and no one wanted to harm them. They just wanted them to go home, stay there for a long time looking at themselves and start thinking about how to behave well. And then they would be welcomed back with open arms, like my Son on the cross when He saved them all, in order to make Chile something more like my Kingdom on Earth. This is my word.

Chapter 35

— What are you doing here?

— Piloting the plane. Can't you see?

— But... you don't know how to fly a plane.

— I am flying it, no? And we have not crashed yet.

— Yet!

— Well, apart from my single practice without a pilot, this is the second time I have been in charge of a flight. We will see what happens. One learns by making mistakes.

— Don't try to be funny with me. I thought I'd hired a serious company.

— Do you really think there is anything serious down there?

— You're a clown.

— What do you want me to be! I was born down there, not up here.

— Good God...! Where did you learn to fly planes?

— I took the opportunity because they offered a free course for commercial aircraft pilots.

— Which generous company is that?

— I don't know if it was a company. It was a group of cheerful and good-natured young Muslims.

— Whaaaaaat?! Young Muslims?

— Don't be prejudiced. What have you got against Muslims? My father was a Muslim.

— And you? Are you one too?

— No, I'm an opportunist.

Fernandísimo Plaza de los Reyes was sweating. He wiped his handkerchief over his face again and again. He was breathing hard. There, in the passenger cabin, Mr. Bob stared indifferently out of the window. He couldn't understand so much limitless blue. Nor did he understand the talking creatures on the plane.

— And... and... what did these "young" Muslims ask you in return for teaching you to be a pilot?

— Nothing. Just to sign some documents.

— And you signed them?

— Of course. I needed the course to make a living. The business of lying, you know, it collapsed.

— And what did those documents say? What did they require you to do?

— I don't know. They were written in Arabic and I don't know how to read that language. My father was illiterate.

— So then...

— So what?

— I don't know... then...

— Well, they told me that they would call me to give me instructions.

— For the love of God! What if they call you and tell you to crash the plane into a building?

— I would not listen to them. Do you think I'm stupid? Can't you see I'm on the plane?

— Do you think we'll arrive safe and sound in New York?

— Nothing has happened so far. Why are you so pessimistic? Why should the rest of the trip be worse than now? You know? Things are changing, but always for the better, even if it doesn't seem so.

— You're a philosopher now.

— Nothing of the kind. I am opportunistic and I think positively. Go and sit down and enjoy the trip. If the plane starts going down, don't worry, I will let you know.

Fernandísimo returned to the passenger cabin. Mr. Bob, seeing him come back, looked up at him and gave him a questioning face. Dogs ask with their eyes. They express many things with their eyes. So when he first saw the birds flying outside the plane window, the dog expressed concern and alarm with his eyes. It was because it was a night of dark nocturnal birds that were hampering the plane's approach to the Big Apple.

Chapter 36

I woke up well past midnight covered in sweat, sitting up suddenly. At my side snoring, as always, was my beautiful Antonieta.

— Wake up.

She made a noise like something from the animal kingdom, turned and continued sleeping. That annoyed me. I hated her for snoring at those moments, that subhuman guttural noise, the damned way she slept so deeply, for not obeying me and waking up, for being my partner in the inheritance left by Fernandísimo Plaza de los Reyes. I hated her as much as that dog that would take the biggest slice of the money. I felt that now was the time to kill her. I had the necessary urge, the desire to do it, the courage to do it, my tie hanging on the back of the chair to strangle her with, but at that time and in that place and in those circumstances it wouldn't have been a good strategy. I decided to postpone the execution. I knew that I still needed her to consummate the main crime. The nightmare I had just had was a forewarning. So I gave her a big slap on her asscheek and shouted in her ear:

— Wake up, slut!

She woke up with a start and howled right in my face:

— What the fuck's going on?

I was about to slap her, but I managed to restrain myself.

— Let's get dressed now! We have to leave for New York.

— What...? At this time? It's four in the morning.

— Who cares what time it is? We have to get to New York as soon as possible. If not, all is lost.

— What's got into you?

— I had a horrible nightmare and it was so real, so vivid and realistic that I'm sure it was a premonition. I dreamed that...

I had to shut up. The room had started to shake. Chile was a country of earthquakes, tsunamis and other disasters worse than politicians. We went pale and our anger was forgotten. We hugged each other seeking protection. The tremor continued, but it was a strong one. We were expecting a sudden shudder from a deadly quake. We remained still, clinging like moss to a rock, feeling that we loved each other, that we had never thought to murder each other, and certainly not for such a vile thing as money. My God, save us, don't take away our lives, which are the most important thing. Nothing else matters. The minutes passed slowly. The earth stopped moving. The fatal quake hadn't come and calm prevailed. We breathed a sigh of relief and, seeing her disheveled in front of me, I hated her again. In turn she bared her teeth at me and barked:

— How can you wake me up at this hour for a stupid nightmare, you idiot!

— Moron, it's not a stupid nightmare! It was a warning, a premonition! Fernandísimo Plaza de los Reyes is going to do something very bad in New York that could leave us without a cent!

At this point Antonieta seemed to start seeing reason.

— What bad thing is he going to do to that'll leave us without the inheritance?

— I've forgotten the details. You know what dreams are like, but I had an alarming feeling. He'll do something that'll mean we don't get a penny.

— Maybe he'll fall in love with one of those gringas who look like dolls and he'll break his word and give his whole fortune to her.

— My nightmare was something like that. A blonde running naked on a bridge and him behind her with a wad of bills in his hand... and I don't know... another bunch of things that I can't remember, but they made me feel like we're about to be disinherited. The last thing in the nightmare was a commanding voice that told me to "get up and walk".

— Isn't that what they said to Lazarus?

— Lazarus? Who's Lazarus?

— It doesn't matter. What do you propose to do?

— Heed the voice, get up and walk.

— I don't understand you.

— Let's get dressed, go to the airport and take the first plane to New York.

— Isn't it too early? It's not even dawn yet.

— It's never too early when joy is about to abandon you.

— Wow! Who said that?

— Me.

— What a disappointment! I thought it was John Lennon.

— Put your clothes on. We have to get the first plane.

— Get the first plane. That only happens in movies.

— Life is a movie. Hurry up.

— But what's the point of going to New York?

— Have you gone dumb or something? We're going to New York to kill Fernandísimo before he does anything that leaves us without the inheritance. And while we're there we'll kill his fucking dog.

— Alright. I'll be ready in ten minutes.

— Better make it five. Don't forget the meat knife. Put it in the luggage.

— Honey, you can't even take weapons on planes in movies now.

— Alright. We'll buy one in New York... or better still in New Jersey, it'll be cheaper.

— But what do you want the knife for?

— What do you mean what for? Have you forgotten why we're going already?! Didn't you ever read "Jack the Ripper"?

Chapter 37

T he first obstacle that presented itself to the new and inexperienced pilot Tarud Arab as he began the approach that would eventually take him to land at New York's John F. Kennedy airport were the birds. Were they eagles? Black plumage, broad and huge wings, powerful white heads, straight beak jutting downwards at a forty-five degree angle. First they skimmed around the plane, then, like an air force squadron they flew ahead like escorts so the pilots could see them. Then hundreds more of these birds flew alongside the plane, almost brushing their wings against the windows. The numbers of these creatures began to multiply to the point of darkening the sky. Visibility was reduced almost to zero and the radar began to fail. Everyone panicked. The cheerful Arabic guys hadn't shown Tarud a flight procedure for such an emergency. Mr. Bob began barking desperately, losing his stiff British upper lip. Fernandísimo tried in vain to remember the Lord's Prayer and from his mouth came a pitiful, mournful and desperate religious gibbering, begging for mercy. The beautiful stewardesses sat in their seats and fastened their safety belts, but that didn't stop them from peeing themselves in fear. In the cockpit, the flight engineer desperately pulled at his thick black beard and invoked Allah in guttural Arabic. The copilot tried to contact the control tower at JFK, but the communication was interrupted by very strange noises and the sounds emitted by the thousands of birds that had suddenly come from out of nowhere. Someone would later point out that, in Brooklyn, in Williamsburg on Broadway, he had seen hundreds and hundreds of birds flying up from the dome of an old building built in 1865, heading towards the sky. No one believed him, since such an outlandish tale didn't inspire much credibility. It was the artist nicknamed "Chile". Tarud Arab clung to the yoke and exclaimed in purest Chilean Spanish: "For fuck's sake and what I do now? What I do now? Fucking son of a bitch!"

Everyone's terror reached a peak when they heard the birds utter words in English. "Go, go home, go back, you are not welcome, this is not your land, this is not your home." They kept repeating the same expressions. They thought they were all going crazy. It couldn't be possible that there were birds flying out there at that altitude obstructing the flight of the aircraft, and worse yet, it was impossible for those birds to be talking. The only one who didn't think he had gone mad was Plaza de los Reyes. He didn't understand what the birds were saying. He could only hear unintelligible noises coming out of their beaks.

— They're speaking English —the cabin chief told him in a trembling voice. Do you realize?

And Fernandísimo replied with a face of uncertainty and confusion.

— In English? Impossible. I speak English. I've studied it for years preparing for the time I went home, but I don't understand the sounds that those damned birds are making out there.

The cabin chief wanted to check if Fernandísimo was telling the truth or not. She addressed him in English.

— What's happening right now is awful!

Fernandísimo cupped a hand to his ear.

— What did you say? I can't understand anything. You're making the same strange sounds as those birds.

The stewardess thought Fernandísimo must be lying about understanding English. Between us, for some strange reason that I won't reveal, all the English that had had been stored in Fernandísimo's brain for so many years had just been erased.

Chapter 38

It happened just like in the movies. When we arrived at the airport in Santiago, after having made the arrangements online, we jumped on the first plane to New York and here we are. We've come to New Jersey, which is very close, just across the Hudson River under the Lincoln Bridge by bus and only five or ten minutes at most, because it's cheaper than New York. We're in Union City in a lousy hotel on 38th Street and Bergenline Avenue. The price per week is laughably low, but what's certainly no laughing matter is the rundown dirtiness of the place, the kind of people you see wandering around inside, men and women of different races but with suspicious appearances. Everything smells of drugs, prostitution, human trafficking and crime. A few seconds ago, Antonieta complained that she didn't like the place I chose, but I replied that it's the right place for two reasons: "One, my dear, is because it's very cheap and the other, honey, is because we're a couple of criminals not far removed from this trash you can see here." And as she shouts at me in response that I'm a worthless moron, I tell her that my idea of having gotten a visa for the United States as soon as we knew of Fernandísimo's intentions didn't indicate that I was a moron, or useless. The matter that we just finished discussing was the most incredible nonsense and internally I feel more and more that I just to get rid of her as soon as possible. But first I need her to cooperate with me in executing that damn dog Bob and its poor master. It's not that I've given up the idea of murdering him; money is money and ensuring my wellbeing is the first duty in my existence, but I've started feeling pity and compassion for Fernandísimo. He's a naïve man, a good man and he's always been kind and generous to us. But without his early death, we, or rather I, could lose a fortune that will make me strong, important and powerful. I never forget my father's words to me when I was about six years old: "In life, son, you always have to be a winner, never a loser, no matter what it costs." No matter what, it can't take more than three days for Fernandísimo Plaza de los Reyes to become a corpse. I passed that sentence a long while ago and now, at this very moment, I'm enforcing it. That's why we're already on the street with Antonieta and walking along Bergenline Avenue, looking to buy a large, sharp knife. It's difficult. Everywhere they say they don't have sharp knives. It seems strange to me. In this great country you have a right to buy yourself weapons of war if you like and they don't sell sharp knives! It must be because they don't know us. We went into the wrong stores. Bergenline Avenue is, by all accounts, a very long avenue covering lots of blocks and where practically all the trade is in the hands of Latinos, Indians, Chinese and anyone but Americans. We're looking where we shouldn't and by speaking Spanish with these people we're somehow betraying who we are. It's essential to meet as few people as possible and speak to practically nobody, in English or in Spanish, find Fernandísimo in Manhattan, execute him with surgical precision, execute the dog and then become Henry VIII of England and execute my Anne Boleyn. Once Antonieta's body has stopped floating and is down on the bed of the East River, I take the plane back and in Chile I await the executor's announcement that I'm the sole heir. What worries me is that my planned crime isn't perfect. It's clear and obvious that Antonieta and I have come to the United States on flight such and such on whatever airline and that we entered the country at New York via JFK on 'x' date at 'x' time. When I go back to Chile, the same evidence will be there. The police will discover the bodies of Fernandísimo, the dog and Antonieta. These gringos have very advanced technology, good search and rescue equipment and unsurpassed divers. The truth is that I have no alibi for all that evidence and the loose ends. But, well, I'm pure Chilean, by birth, race and upbringing and, as such, we shall see. I'll cross that bridge when I come to it and, anyway, I've always been saved by the bell at the last minute. And I'm a man of faith. I know that God is with me. I've never been behind with my church tithes.

As I was saying! Providence is with me, well, in the end, something is with me. "Antonieta, as you're carrying that big bag, get that knife that we've been looking for from the trashcan. Can you see it? Someone threw it in there for some reason. Maybe it was a criminal running away. It's just what we need. Look, Antonieta, a big, sharp meat knife. Come on, hurry up, there's no one coming. Lean into the trashcan, grab it and hide it in the bag. Good, well done! Now, let's go. Let's take the bus to New York, the Bergenline Number 159 is good, it leaves us in Manhattan, at the Port Authority, right on 8th Avenue with 42nd Street. That's where we'll be, Antonieta, three blocks or so from Times Square, right in the middle of Broadway. From there we take 7th Avenue uptown, we cross the street where Carnegie Hall is. Have you ever heard of Carnegie Hall? And we get to Central Park. He'll be there, or he already is, our victim and generous benefactor, staying at one of the most luxurious hotels in the Big Apple. Come on sweetheart, so we can scout the place out and follow his tracks until we can strike. I feel like a fictional character, don't you? Or rather, I feel like the author of my own novel, like a demiurge who weaves his own destiny and that of others. I feel like the world is mine, that now I'm the one who controls things... Look, here comes the 159 and we're right at the stop. Tell him to stop. Well, thank you, my darling. At last you're obedient. This northern hemisphere air suits you. Here it comes. Too bad we're still so young. We're not entitled to the Senior Citizen, round-trip fare. Just imagine, it would've been so cheap for us: three dollars and a dime each, there and back."

Chapter 39

Tarud Arab thought that this, being his first flight as captain, he would soon become a martyr of commercial aviation. The news would reverberate around the world because of the unusual situation and the fatal accident that appeared to be about to take place. The birds were already filling the entire sky. It was an immense carpet of black birds flying lower than the plane's altitude, making the ground invisible. The radars weren't working. Radio communication had been cut off. He was flying blind, not knowing if the city of New York was already down there and he had the feeling that the birds were somehow guiding the plane despite his efforts. The copilot could only manage to say, "this is a paranormal phenomenon." The flight engineer, still with his hands clutching his black thick beard, repeated: "If Allah wills is, then so be it." Tarud Arab answered him, asking: "And can you find out what the hell Allah wants?" For his part, Fernandísimo Plaza de los Reyes hugged Mr. Bob and repeated: "My whole fortune for just a few more years of life!" The stewardesses, holding hands, recited the Lord's Prayer with a devotion that surprised even them.

And then the shudders began. One after another and then increasingly strong. The structure creaked as if it would be torn to shreds at any instant. The interior lights flickered and the plane was plunged into darkness for what seemed like an eternity. With a supreme effort, Tarud Arab tried to focus his attention on what he saw outside. Down below he could saw only a layer of black. The birds. Up above, he could see that the sky was clear and full of stars. He felt as if there was hope up there and that death was the only possibility below. But how could he climb higher? Impossible. The plane could do no more. Its ceiling was limited. To get any higher it would have to be an entity made with very different materials. More than mere chemistry and physics, it would have to be some magical alchemy. But it was just a machine made by the prestigious aviation company Boeing.

Suddenly the radio began to crackle. Words in English. No, it wasn't the English of the birds. It was the voice of an official air traffic controller at JFK airport. He identified the flight, gave the precise coordinates, informed them of the weather, fog with almost zero visibility, indicated the available runway, began guiding the plane and authorized it to land. Everyone's souls returned to their bodies and even more so when they looked outside and saw that the birds had all disappeared. Of course, they couldn't see New York either or the runway. Everything had vanished under a thick veil of mist that was clinging to the ground. However, between the radars and the human voice of the air traffic controllers, the plane managed to land on the runway, rolled the distance it had to roll, taxied it to its final place of arrival and stopped. The engines fell silent. They were safe at JFK, although they couldn't even spot the airport through the fog. But there they were. Had a miracle happened despite what was possibly a curse?

When Fernandísimo got off the plane, he moved through the jet bridge into the building and, noticing that nothing could be seen due to the mist, he exclaimed:

— Wow, I'm not home yet! I can't see anything. I'm in the middle of a cloud of steam. Where's the airport, where's my beloved New York?

Beside him, Arab replied:

— You must be dreaming. There's no fog in here. Everything is bright and clear. We're in the JFK buildings and you have to hand over your documentation. Maybe your blindness is a result of the shock of what we just experienced.

— I don't know, I don't know, I don't know. I can't see anything. Not you, or anyone else. I'm inside a cloud. Can it be that I'm dying? Is this how one dies from colonic cancer? Can anyone see a doctor to ask?

They couldn't help but laugh. But they did so decently, discreetly. After all, they all must have gone crazy or been delirious or something, they thought. They had seen birds outside the plane and they were speaking in English. Birds fly, or at least most of them do, and for them to hamper the flight of a plane is almost sanely credible, but birds that speak English is something only for movies or novels. They helped him hand over his papers. The long process had at last been completed. The luxury car that the hotel had sent arrived immediately and departed for Manhattan to fill the reservations made at the five-star The Mark, less than a mile from Central Park on Madison Avenue and 77ᵗʰ Street. Most importantly, Mr. Bob would have no problems, as the hotel accepted guests with pets. As the car cruised along the highway and then through the streets of Brooklyn, crossed the East River over the Williamsburg Bridge and finally rolled through the streets of colossal Manhattan, Fernandísimo Plaza de los Reyes was unable to enjoy the things that the flight attendants, the blond copilot, the bearded flight engineer, and the cheerful Tarud Arab could see through the windows. He still felt that he was within a cloud that enveloped him and his eyes could only see mist, thick fog, white as cotton or blinding snow, but with black consequences.

The finally arrived at The Mark Hotel. The protocols were fulfilled. They checked in, the bellboys took the luggage up to the suite and with Fernandísimo still unable to appreciate anything. Fog, fog, blindness. He just heard voices, noises, strident music and those voices. He heard words he couldn't understand like those spoken by the birds during the nightmare flight. Fortunately Tarud Arab took over for him. He did everything and when he finally left Fernandísimo sitting on a comfortable couch in his suite, he withdrew, saying:

— Mr. Plaza de los Reyes, don't worry about anything. I will stay in my room and will be prepared for anything you need. I'll call a doctor right away to see if we can solve your blindness. If you'll excuse me.

As soon as he heard the door close, Fernandísimo thought out loud: "After all, that liar with the turban doesn't seem to be such a bad man." And then he couldn't stand it any longer and began sobbing. He had been so hopeful, so sure of his return home and then to go through he was experiencing. The birds, the blindness of the cloud that was keeping him isolated. How awful, to be standing in New York and yet not be in New York. How desperate not to be able to see it, not to take in the bright Manhattan night. He could only hear, and what he heard was just deafening noise, chaotic symphonies, strident disharmonies and a language of angry birds that he couldn't understand. My God, what is all this?! And as slowly as the cunning advance of a snake, the sobs gradually diminished until they disappeared and then came sleep, the sleep of opium and after the silence of forgotten cemeteries he fell deep asleep with shadows clouding his mind.

The distant sound of a cheerful military march awakened him. It was a band that seemed to be playing inside the room, but at the same time from a very distant dimension. He felt that the march was touching him in particular. But who, where, why him? He lay still for a long time, not yet opening his eyes, reveling in those martial, optimistic, cheerful sounds. Might they be paying him homage? Could they be welcoming him? Welcoming him to where, New York? Had he finally made it home? Very slowly he opened his eyes and he couldn't believe it. He could see. The cloud had gone. There he was, sitting on that springy and luxurious sofa in the middle of a suite fit for royalty. Well, despite everything, he was a Plaza de los Reyes. He took a deep breath and was filled with a sense of wellbeing and immense contentment. He almost jumped to his feet and went to one of the windows, peering out. The first thing he thought he saw was something like a white dove flying away, up towards the skyscrapers. Do doves fly that high? Out there the Big Apple flashed in multicolor, the city that never sleeps, the New York he loved.

Chapter 40

The band continued playing. Was it in his ear? Maybe inside his head? Out in the street? In another room? He had entered a state of complete vigilance and lucidity. He looked out of the window again. He wanted to see if the band was playing outside. No, nothing. He put his ear against the walls. Nothing on the other side. He opened the door of the suite. The hallway outside was silent. He closed the door and the band started to play again. A welcome melody? He checked the TV. Silent, no sound, no picture. That martial music had to be coming from nowhere, brilliant, joyful and hopeful. Maybe it was no actual part of the Earth's surface; it was coming from some distant dimension. He heard the band as if in the background from a very distant time and a time not existing on this earthly plane. "No, I can't be hallucinating" —he said— "That's the last thing I need." He wanted to pick up the intercom, call reception and ask if there might be any piped music in the hotel that was playing military marches. He was just about to do so when he remembered that his knowledge of English had vanished from his head. He sat frustrated. Too many strange things were happening to him, outside of all logic and normality. The music attracted his attention once again and his contentment returned. That march was telling him something, something was being announced. Was it good? Hopeful? A sure promise? An infinite optimism brightened him from within inside. Would his cancer be cured? He was in New York. Now he didn't want to die in New York anymore. On the contrary, He wanted to live in New York and hopefully forever. "Is that what this welcome band is telling me? Blessed be God!" But a shrill and threatening sound like a squawk shook him violently from his state of bliss. He glanced instantly at the place where the noise had come from. He felt his heart miss a beat and a sense of horror darkened his soul. There, on top of an elegant bronze and silver floor lamp, with baroque reliefs with pastoral figures, was a huge black bird, just like those that had attacked his flight to New York. When Fernandísimo looked at it, the bird opened its wings and spread its feathers in a sign of attack. It made another terrifying sound, but this time, Fernandísimo understood the vocal message. The bird seemed to scream in a savage shriek: "Go home, go home." He was just beginning to realize that he seemed to have regained his knowledge of English, when the bird took flight around the suite, flapping with its wings at the curtains, lamps, glasses, porcelain ornaments, pictures hanging on the walls, knocking everything down, breaking things and, in the midst of that hellish confusion, came the most chilling cry of terror ever emitted from the mouth of Fernandísimo when he saw that monster with its powerful wings and beak flying directly towards him.

Chapter 41

— The caves of Altamira and Lascaux.

— What?

— That's where the secret is. First they drew what they wanted to happen and then it happened afterwards thanks to that.

— Does that have anything to do with killing Fernandísimo and Mr. Bob? Or are you feverish?

— Lower your voice, they can hear you.

— I'm speaking Spanish, what are they going to understand?!

— There are lots of people here who speak Spanish.

— So?

— What?

— Something about some caves...

— Oh yeah.

I'm leaning over an art history book in one of the majestic halls of The Public Library of New York on 5th Avenue and 42nd Street.

— From what I read in these books, what I've been doing has been perfect.

— Are you trying to be mysterious with me?

I look her in the eye and reproach her for her constant irony. My fatigue has reached its limit and I decide right then that not many more days will go by without her becoming a corpse. I'm steeling my patience so I answer with feigned calm.

— In these books they talk about the first cave paintings in prehistory. They were found in the caves of Altamira in the Cantabria region of Spain and in the Lascaux cave in France. They're mainly hunting scenes with surprising colors and realism. Look at the pictures.

She leans over to look at them, puts on her glasses, but she doesn't even say "Oh!"

— It's thought that before leaving to hunt, those prehistoric men first drew the act of hunting with the animal already the victim of his spear. That way they ensured that the hunt would be propitiatory. By drawing what they intended to do, the future was decreed. It was a propitiatory magic.

— But I think that's pure nonsense. The people who discovered those caves, how would they know why those prehistoric guys drew all those monkeys! Hahaha... They probably didn't even draw them in prehistoric times.

— You have to believe in something in this world. If not how can I let a barber shave me when he puts his razor against my throat? I need to believe that he's not thinking about cutting my jugular... Antonieta, you can't be that foolish!

— Well okay. And so what? Did you draw that dog Bob and Fernandísimo with his guts hanging out?

— How disgusting! Never so gross! Come on, let's go back to New Jersey to the hotel. I'll show you my genius.

We get up. I hand the book in. We hurry down the stairs, we get to 42nd Street, we turn left and we're heading at a rapid pace to Port Authority to take the 159 bus that leaves us in Union City. Here on Avenue of the Americas the traffic light stops us. There's too much traffic. Finally we're crossing.

— Hurry up. I'm anxious to show her my propitiatory magic. Look over there. We're in front of Times Square already. Look, there's a whole bunch of musicals on. When we finish what we've planned, we'll celebrate by going to see "An American in Paris". Then we'll go to Paris and from Paris to London and from there to wherever we choose. It'll all begin for us, Antonieta, the great life... happiness at last!

Chapter 42

We're in our room of our modest hotel in Union City, New Jersey.

— Read this.

— What I've written. It's propitiatory magic. It doesn't work just by drawing. I'd say it's better to write. Don't forget: "And in the beginning was the word..." It seems that when God named things he created them. He said, "Let there be light, and there was light."

— I didn't know you had that skill.

— You never know who the person beside you really is. Come on, read.

Antonieta begins to read. I see her frown. She looks astonished. Now she stares at me.

— But what is this?

— I told you. Propitiatory magic.

— What kind of propitiatory magic? You wrote what happened to us at the lake, our clothes getting stolen, the nightmare with the guys in the truck, our fight with them, the way we killed them... so, what kind of propitiatory magic? You wrote down everything that happened to us.

— I wrote it down before it happened to us.

— What?!

— That's right. One day I had the idea of writing a novel about us...

— You, for God's sake? When have you been a writer?

— Never before. But one day I woke up a writer and I had the urge to write. The one who awakes isn't always the one who goes to sleep the night before. Even you, did you imagine as a teenager that one day you were going to wake up with a criminal mentality?

— Shut up, will you?

— The thing is that suddenly I realized that what I wrote soon happened to us in real life. With the word we can create our own destiny.

— And why the hell did you come up with the idea of murders and imagining us as the real monsters we are now?

— I don't know. Maybe I've had that monster inside since I was born. I don't know. I wrote what came into my head and, on the other hand, what I consciously want for our lives. I write…

— Let me guess, you wrote about being the heirs of Fernandísimo Plaza de los Reyes?

— Naturally.

— And why the fuck did it occur to you to write that the old man was only going to leave us a part of his fortune while the dog gets the best part? Are you dumb or what?

— I don't know if I am. But I do know that I like a life with risks and adventures. Coming to New York to murder an old millionaire and his equally millionaire dog is still exciting. It practically makes us characters in a novel.

— And what's the advantage of being characters in a novel?

— Well, from there you can become movie characters.

— So what?

— Well, you become more famous. And everything you do doesn't have consequences in the real world. Dying in a novel or in a movie isn't the same as dying in real life. Every time someone opens the book you live again until the end arrives. The same thing every time they watch the movie. Imagine, how many times the bad guy dies in a movie and how many times he lives again, every time the movie is shown!

— Are you sure you don't have a fever? What were the last pills you took?

— Whatever. What I write is coming true. I'm some kind of God. I have the reins of our destinies and of anyone I invent in what I write. Propitiatory magic!

— I'll have to go along with you. What else am I supposed to do! I seem to be in your hands. I hope you write that I end up being the Queen of Sheba and you a crazy lover at my feet.

I smile and look down. I don't dare look into her eyes. I take my text away. It's not in my best interests for her to continue reading.

Chapter 43

Shocked by the cry of terror, Tarud Arab rushed to the room of Fernandísimo Plaza de los Reyes and crashed in through the door. The first thing he saw was a lot of black feathers scattered across the floor and then glass, paintings, lamps, vases, pots, rugs, cushions, armchairs and couches all equally destroyed by the beak of an enormous bird. This was a disaster of destruction and violence. Tarud Arab moved cautiously into the suite. He realized that there was a bird there and that creature somehow had to be one of the same ones that attacked his plane. Very slowly he moved his head from side to side and looked up at the ceiling. He couldn't see what he was afraid to find. Worse still, he couldn't see the millionaire anywhere either. He didn't want to think. He knew that the mind creates fantasies and that these fantasies often became real. In his simple, but cunning brain he realized that the mind creates nightmares and that those nightmares become real and tortuous to those who think of them. He knew by intuition that the world is neither good nor bad and that it is our own minds that transform it into paradise or hell. That's why he refused to think that perhaps the sinister bird had grabbed Fernandísimo Plaza de los Reyes with its mighty beak and taken him away to dark skies. He felt that he cared about the millionaire and was surprised at himself. He realized at that instant that he felt pity, sympathy and concern for the man and not just because of his millions, but because he was a person, no more and no less. Amongst his fear, confusion and restlessness he felt a pleasant sensation about himself. When all was said and done, he wasn't such a son of a bitch as he always thought he was or he'd been made to seem. What miracle was going on within him? He was willing to give what little he had so long as nothing had happened to the poor old man. And at last, after years of forgetfulness, he said my name. Accustomed to business, to transactions, the old 'I'll give you this if you give me that', he gave me human characteristics and said: "Oh God, I give up everything I have, I offer it to you if you save Fernandísimo."

A terrifying scream made him jump. The huge bird was on the curtain rod. It spread its wings and took off. But this time, it flew out of the window and was lost in the nocturnal blue of brightly-lit Manhattan. Tarud Arab rushed to the window and yelled at it: "Where is Mr. Plaza de los Reyes, you hellish bird?"

— I'm here —replied Fernandísimo.

Arab turned around and saw Plaza de los Reyes emerge from the closet. He was disheveled, his clothes ripped and he had wounds on his hands and arms that were bleeding profusely.

— Praise be to God! Mr. Plaza de los Reyes... what a relief... I thought I would never see you again!

— You almost didn't see me again, my friend. That bird nearly killed me. Something turned me into a warrior and I held it at bay with my hands and fists... I don't know... "someone" seemed to put me in the closet just in time.

— All of these things that are happening are very strange.

— What do you want me to say! Everything that's going on tells me that there's no place in the world where you can live in peace and happiness. The planet is inhospitable, isn't it?

— Maybe. I have not seen it all.

— You don't need to. Read history, watch the news.

— But I'm very happy that you're safe and sound despite your injuries. I shall have a doctor come.

— Thank you, Mr. Arab. You are a gentleman after all.

Tarud Arab didn't much like that "after all". He didn't reply. He let it pass. It just caused him a little discomfort.

— There is something that worries me. I don't know if you can answer me.

— Tell me. I don't have the answers to everything, but for a few things perhaps.

— When you offer something to God on the condition that He grants us a favor and He grants it, is it strictly necessary to give Him what you offered Him?

Chapter 44

We're back at the cheap hotel in New Jersey. I finished writing another chapter of the novel. Or rather, my propitiatory text. I show it to Antonieta.

— Come on, read the last part I wrote. This is what's going to happen and it's going to happen to us. Things are coming to a head. The novel is about to end and it'll be a happy ending for us. After that, no more words. Just straight reality, action, facts, wealth, enjoyment. But what is written is being fulfilled. Read it.

Antonieta is looking at me right now. I'm giving her the book. She takes it and flicks through it.

— Don't flip through it. Read it. It's exactly what's going to happen in a few hours. That's for sure.

Now she's beginning to read.

— No Please. Not in silence. Read it out loud. I want to hear how it sounds, how the events will be... here, from this part.

Antonieta has begun to read aloud:

— It was already sunset. We decided to take the bus to Manhattan and so we did. The plan was drawn up and the alibi seemed perfect. We knew exactly where Fernandísimo Plaza de los Reyes was staying: The Mark Hotel, Madison Avenue and 77th Street, room 520. We knew that he was accompanied by that Tarud Arab by some strange circumstance, a man with a turban and who seemed to have been the lover of the missing Madame Chantal, the fortuneteller who deceived Fernandísimo with her lies. We also knew our man's habits: the time he usually walked around Manhattan, what time he returned to the hotel, when he took the dog for a walk. In short, all the details provided by our discreet and meticulous intelligence work. We arrived at Port Authority around 8:00 p.m. A light drizzle was falling. We bought some umbrellas on the corner of 8th Avenue and 42nd Street. We decided to go to the hotel on foot. You walk a lot in New York. New Yorkers often walk dozens of blocks. We did too. But we did it because of a strategic need. We had to find the right homeless guy. Not just anyone. It had to be someone really run down, someone who was homeless due to the effects of drugs, bad habits, being a fugitive from justice. We needed this so we could get him to murder Fernandísimo. We would give him the knife, we would give him the instructions, the location of our victim, the characteristics of the dog and we would offer him a sum of money that we would never pay, because we wouldn't see him again. We would disappear. He would kill our benefactor, he would be caught by the police and we would wait in Chile to hear the good news about the murder of our friend and that we were the heirs to his full fortune. We walked several blocks. By now the night was blackening the sky and Manhattan was providing glamorous illumination. Suddenly, our man appeared. He was a young, blond guy, with typical blue eyes and he was filthy. He was practically lying on the sidewalk with his back against the wall of an old building. What interested me about his eyes wasn't their color but the glassy look and the perversity they expressed. There, in that human debris there was plenty of drugs in his brain and much evil in his heart. He was exactly the right guy, I had no doubt. I spoke to him. At first he seemed not to hear or understand me. Either my English was very poor or he'd forgotten his own English, or he was just totally wasted. At last we managed to communicate. I said:

— If you're capable of killing a guy and his dog with this knife, you can get rich in less than an hour.

I handed him a wad of bills. It was a thousand dollars. He grabbed it in one swipe.

— This is just an advance. Once you've completed your mission, there'll be three million dollars for you.

He tried to stare at me. He remained silent for a long time. Then he said, mumbling with an accent that I found hard to understand.

— It's a deal. How do I have to do it?

— In about half an hour, the man will leave the hotel, and he'll leave with his dog. You go ahead however you like. We'll be watching from here, hidden behind this container. The important thing is that the animal and the man are as dead as possible. No resurrections.

Then I gave him the details. His interest in the money had apparently woken the poor guy right up because I noticed that he was repeating all the information I gave him accurately so he wouldn't forget and could do his job properly. When I'd finished giving him his instructions, we all waited. At almost exactly the right time, we saw Fernandísimo leaving the hotel with Mr. Bob. Everything was propitiatory. Half a block down, the street was dark. Something had happened because the streetlamp wasn't lit.

—It's your time —I told the homeless guy.

The guy put his thousand dollars in the pocket of his shabby blue jeans, clutched the knife and ran across the street. He surprised Fernandísimo with his pet in the darkest part. Like a beast attacking with all the force of its murderous instinct, he buried the knife below the back of our benefactor's neck. He didn't even have time to cry out. A powerful jet of blood shot out, spraying the homeless man right in the face and he fell to the ground without any further fanfare. Only in the movies is death a choreographic process and an attractive and entertaining spectacle. In real life it's simple, instantaneous, without any commotion or aesthetics. It's even less spectacular than birth. On alert, Mr. Bob barked furiously, but the bum slashed his belly and the animal, like his master, fell onto the sidewalk in a large pool of shared blood. The blood of master and pet merged in their last instants on this earth. The hobo immediately ran back to where we were hiding with Antonieta.

— Quick, honey. Let's get away. Mission accomplished.

And we sped far away from the homeless guy who shouted at us like crazy, but he couldn't keep up because he was too weak and unstable. A new life full of light and splendor, consummate with riches and pleasures, was opened up to toward a future of which we could never have dreamed just a few years ago.

Antonieta finishes reading. She says:

— Horrible, but wonderful.

— That's what's going to happen today, just as I wrote it. Let's get going.

Chapter 45

Mr. Bob looks anxious. He knows it's time to go for a walk with his master but he can see that there's no sign of heading outside. It's already night, the suite is dimly lit and in comes Tarud Arab. He has started talking to his master. So Mr. Bob simply yawns.

— You look worried, Arab. It something up? If it's about me, then I appreciate it. I've already recovered from my wounds.

— It's about me, Mr. Plaza de los Reyes.

— Might I ask what's happened to you?

— Of course. That's what I came for. To tell you.

— I'm listening with my ears pricked and my heart open.

— You're a great guy, Mr. Plaza de los Reyes.

— Thank you. So?

— I'm in big trouble. And on the other hand I'm now so poor that I'll have to sleep under the bridges of the Mapocho. That is, if I can make it back to Chile.

— Oh dear. Tell me the details, please.

Tarud Arab made a gesture asking permission to sit. Fernandísimo replied with a nod.

— It's the nice young Arabs who taught me how to be a pilot and they later recommended that an aviation company hire me. The same company whose services you hired.

— I thought so. And what's up with those "nice young Arabs"?

— They called me and put a machine gun to my chest.

— That sounds serious.

— They told me that they are the owners of the company and that the offices and employees are just a facade.

Arab broke off. He was silent, absorbed by his fears.

— And?

— They have threatened to kill me. I have been ordered to fly the plane and crash it into a building.

— Good heavens! Into which building?

— It seems that they're not sure yet. It might be one here in the United States or in another country. They spoke to me about France, Belgium or the United Kingdom. They will tell me in due time.

— What an extraordinary organization!

— They warned me that they're watching me, that several of them are following me and that if I tell anyone about this I'm a dead man. The same if I don't follow the order to crash the plane. They underlined it to me: "You're a dead man either way. If you crash the plane you die. If the plane doesn't crash or you talk about it with someone else, you'll die from our bullets.

— But you're telling me, man! You're taking a risk, aren't you?

— I can't imagine that the dog is a spy —and he glanced at Mr. Bob. The dog lay down, resting his head on the ground and looked up at Arab, giving him a look of canine tenderness.

—And I trust you completely. I don't know why, but I trust you absolutely.

There was a long silence. Fernandísimo Plaza de los Reyes stopped to think deeply. He stared at the ceiling and even beyond, as if seeing the stars through the roof. Arab added in a sudden exclamation.

— I don't want to die! I don't want to die, Mr. Fernandísimo!

The millionaire looked right at him.

— What did you say to those men?

— That I would never crash that plane into anything and they should go to hell.

Fernandísimo smiled at him with affection and a look of complete complacency.

— Good for you, Arab. You won't die, I assure you.

Arab fell to his knees and kissed Fernandísimo's hands profusely.

— My great lord. I knew you would save me. I saw your generosity. I thank you... thank you. With money you can placate those criminals... thank you a thousand times... I swear I will give that money for my ransom back to you, every single cent... I knew it, money can buy anything.

Fernandísimo invited him to stand up.

— Look, Arab, the money in the fund won't buy anyone. You buy people or goods and you become more dispossessed than you were before.

— I don't understand you, sir.

— You will understand me in due time.

— Yes, yes... I hope so.

— By the way, was that broad legal power I gave you any use?

— Yes of course.

— Then you were able to take it all out, absolutely all my bank assets?

— I took out all your money, paying taxes, interest and other costs. I had to rent a security company with an armored car to bring so many bags loaded with bills to the hotel. They are all in my room, better hidden than in the cave of Ali Baba and the forty thieves.

— Perfect. Thank you, Tarud. You're very efficient and a good man, as I have just verified.

— I have been liar and a con artist my whole life.

— We're all liars and con artists more than once in our lives. What do you want?! Do you think that an elephant can have a brain other than that of an elephant?

— I don't think so.

— Well, men can't have any other brain than a human brain. Do you understand?

— No.

— It doesn't matter. Look outside. It looks like some of the street lamps have been burned out.

— Yes, it does.

— Arab, please, come with me. Let's take Mr. Bob out for a walk. He's already impatient.

And after a happy bark with which Mr. Bob gave his approval, the three of them went out into the Manhattan night.

Chapter 46

Antonieta and I are on our way to our objective. We've stopped on the corner to wait for the bus, which is taking too long to arrive as far as I can tell.

— This bus is too late —says Antonieta. We won't make it in time to get there when Fernandísimo takes the dog for a walk.

I reply uneasily:

— It's true. That never happens with these buses. It doesn't happen with the small buses of the private companies either.

— I see that things aren't starting to happen like you wrote them.

— I'm getting edgy —I answer— Take it easy. Propitiatory magic never fails. These are just details. The details can vary. The important thing always happens.

Antonieta has folded her arms. I notice she's looking at me. Possibly mockingly? I'm going to ignore it.

— What do we do? —she asks.

I tell her we'd better take a taxi.

— But that's very expensive.

— It doesn't matter as long as we get there on time. What's a New Jersey taxi fare to New York compared to the millions we're going to inherit?

There's a taxi. I make him stop and we're getting in. I close the door. I give the address to the driver and the car pulls away.

— This isn't very similar to what you wrote.

— I insist. The details may vary. The important things won't change.

We move forward. We're already crossing the Hudson River over the Lincoln Bridge. There's not much traffic. In a few minutes we arrive at Port Authority. Considering the time, I ask the driver not to drop us there but near The Mark Hotel.

— Another detail wrong —Antonieta exclaims. Where's your propitiatory magic? We were supposed to get off at Port Authority and buy an umbrella there because it started to drizzle and now it turns out that we're going to arrive by taxi at the meeting place. There's bright sunshine and we haven't bought a fucking umbrella!

— I must insist again. The details vary, but...

— I know, the important thing is the same.

— Don't make fun of me, Antonieta.

The driver looks at us in the mirror and speaks.

— Excuse me for being nosy. I heard what you were saying without wanting to. I know a little about propitiatory magic. I belong to an esoteric study group.

— Wonderful! I'm telling her about it now.

— And as I was saying, I usually write stories. I wrote one in which a real guy, who was very unpleasant to me and who had caused me serious problems in my life, takes a plane and the plane crashes. Everyone is saved and he's the only one who dies. As it turned out, in reality, the guy boarded the plane and the things I wrote were basically fulfilled. The plane crashed and they all died, the crew and all the passengers. The only one that was saved was him. But as you can see, these are details. The plane crashed and I think he's done very badly in life. I'm satisfied with that. We're here. That's a hundred and fifty dollars.

We're getting out of the taxi. In a bad mood I pay the fare. Too expensive. The driving writer leaves with his taxi. I'm prepared to complain, but now I have a happy face. Right there is the homeless guy just as I described him.

— What did I tell you, Antonieta!

— Oh, I see your propitiatory magic has started working.

We rush towards the guy. I'm talking to him...

— ...there's a thousand dollars for you...

The guy snatches them out of my hand.

— Just as it's written —Antonieta whispers in my ear, excited, happy, hopeful.

I'm explaining to the guy what he has to do. Now he's expressing his willingness to me, just as I'd written in the novel. And just like was written, I hand him the knife. We watch and see the trio leaving the hotel.

— But that guy with the turban doesn't appear in your novel right now. Fernandísimo is supposed to be alone with the dog.

— Well, Antonieta. Details. Let the important thing happen.

Antonieta opens her eyes even more bewildered.

— Look what just happened. The lights just came on. Someone must have fixed them. In the novel the street is dark. Things are starting to go wrong, Ricardo.

— No, the important thing is about to begin now. Trust me.

I look at the homeless guy and signal at him to move into action.

— Ok, buddy, do your thing. If you have to kill all three, then do it. The pay is triple.

The homeless guy heeds me immediately. He springs up and like an angry bull crosses the street towards them. It looks like Fernandísimo, the man with the turban and the dog haven't noticed anything.

— Let's watch, Antonieta. Look at him running. He'll reach them in a second.

— Oh, yeah, how exciting!

— You'll see how he'll stab them all. Don't be shocked by the blood you're about to see. It's part of this business.

We hear a bark, then several more, repeated, aggressive, defensive.

— That wasn't written, Ricardo.

I didn't write what I'm seeing now either. The homeless guy is trying to calm the dog. Fernandísimo manages to settle him down.

— Ricardo, by God, that bum is thanking Fernandísimo. They're smiling.

I can't believe what I'm seeing right now. The homeless guy pulls something out of his pocket and shows him, I don't know what... it looks like an ID card or something...

— Ricardo, don't tell me he's a cop. Damn your propitiatory magic, you asshole!

I can see them speak. The man with the turban looks astonished. The homeless guy points at us with his finger. Something is certainly going wrong. Those damned creatures aren't doing what they're told.

— Ricardo, let's run. They're coming.

The dog comes running towards us, barking like an enraged beast and behind him is the homeless man, the guy with the turban and Fernandísimo following swiftly behind. I never thought the old man could run at that speed. I never imagined or conceived it like that. We speed away, followed too closely behind. We hear the voice of the homeless guy who shouts at us in an authoritarian and clear and cultured English: "Stop. This is the police" And a shot into the air makes us run even faster.

Chapter 47

Things have to come to an end, not as men plan them more often than not, but as they really have to come to an end. Although the world is a big lie, not everything in the world is a lie.

Things happened in expected ways. The thing is that Mr. Bob, his master, Tarud Arab, the homeless man named Fred, who worked as an undercover police officer and was now in uniform, were in the suite of the hotel where Fernandísimo was staying. Cuffed to one another were Antonieta and Ricardo.

— Who would've thought it! My heirs, the potential murderers of their own benefactor.

— The truth is that we....

— You'd better not say anything, Antonieta. Any explanation will make it worse.

— Yes, of course... sorry.

— Who would've thought it! The country I loved the most in the world welcomes me with sinister birds, it hides from me with a sinister fog, it twists my ears with English I can't understand, denies me residence papers, and so on and so on.

Fred the cop tries to be nice.

— My country respects freedom and people's rights. But it also respects its own rules. Calmly and patiently, taking the right steps, I'm sure that the United States of America will become your home.

Fernandísimo smiled at them all with a wise expression.

— To tell you the truth, the whole planet should be home to each and every one of us. But it's not.

— Why do you say that? —asked Tarud Arab.

— Because, as I said before, Arab, elephants can only have elephant brains and humans can only have human brains.

— I'm still wondering what that means.

— Look, don't get dizzy or believe in mirages when you see the science and technology, the arts and philosophy that creates man. Don't think that's progress. Man hasn't advanced a step from his status as primitive man. Wars have never finished and armies are increasingly efficient at killing more people at a lower cost and in less time. Men only know how to fuck one another, never love one another. Our brains aren't made to do that. We'd have to be born again. And no one is an exception from that. We're all equally violent and the enemies of our fellow men. It's just that some are like that in one way and others in another.

They all looked at each other. There were murmurs, comments, and then another silence as they waited for Fernandísimo to continue speaking.

— First of all, I want to thank the police officer who has agreed to bring his prisoners with me. I promised to make them my heirs and, in spite of everything, I won't let them down.

Antonieta and Ricardo looked at each other and a glimmer of hope softened the expression of dejection in their eyes.

— Arab, is everything in the car?

— That's right, Mr. Plaza de los Reyes. Everything is just as you arranged it.

— Very well. Let's all go to Brooklyn Bridge. It's a good place and the night is starry enough to celebrate life. Officer, if you could take the cuffs off my heirs, they will be more comfortable and a little happier. I don't want anyone around me feeling sorrow and slavery.

As a good man, experienced in the struggle for respect, order and honesty, Fred understood. He removed the handcuffs from the young husband and wife. Ricardo and Antonieta thanked the policeman, their great benefactor and even the dog, which, when they looked at him, turned his head as a sign of disaffection. Antonieta went further and kissed Fernandísimo on the cheek. He thought, but didn't say, "that's definitely the kiss of Judas."

— Let's go, my friends —said Plaza de los Reyes.

Everyone went out after him. The car drove them to the Brooklyn Bridge. It was a Manhattan night and down the river from that beautiful work of engineering you could see the towering Statue of Liberty lit up in the distance. It was like an unparalleled leader, guiding not only the United States, but the whole world to more elevated horizons.

The car stopped in the middle of the bridge. It was nighttime by now and there was no traffic. Fernandísimo got out. The others did the same. No one had any idea of what was about to happen. The millionaire raised both arms above him.

— This, my friends, is the ritual of dying in New York. This is what I came for. After my death I will be reborn. That's why I am on this iconic, historic bridge of undeniable beauty. Every bridge joins two points and crosses deep and uncertain waters. I will jump to my death and towards rebirth.

Everyone become concerned. Fred, the policeman, warned him very diplomatically that he wouldn't let him commit suicide. He was the representative of the law and such an act was illegal. Fernandísimo replied what I whispered into his ear from within:

— Officer, it's not suicide. It's just lifting my feet off this planet. And not only my feet, but also my heart and my mind.

— Don't do anything to yourself, Fernandísimo —begged Antonieta.

— Calm down, I would never do anything to myself. And don't worry. Neither you nor your husband will be disinherited. It will all depend on you whether you're rich or poor.

Fernandísimo looked toward the Statue of Liberty. It radiated light and magical prescience.

— Lady of hope, lady of the highest dignity and respect that God teaches us for one to another, beacon, which on the shifting waters of existence illuminates the road to a true homeland, I respect you, I hear you, I follow you.

Then he gave an order to Arab.

— Tarud, help me.

And then came his great act of freedom. They opened the big trunk of the car and between them they began throwing bags full of hundreds and millions of dollars one by one like excited children. Mr. Bob celebrated the ritual by barking happily, doing pirouettes and standing on his two hind legs. In unison Ricardo and Antonia made two terrifying cries of despair, of rage, of fury, of unrestrained violence. Fred, the police officer, scratched his head and couldn't understand anything. The bags fell noisily onto the water of the Hudson. The river swirled in surprised and unexpected ripples and waves. Some bags dropped quickly, straight to the bottom. Others floated as if not wanting to lose the power of manipulating men. When the last bag fell into the water, the whine of a marine siren could be heard. Was it a sound of celebration? Was it one of sadness and regret? It was at that moment that Antonieta and Ricardo made the decision of their lives. They suddenly climbed the railing of the bridge and leapt towards the water. They fell heavily and their bodies disappeared beneath the surface. Endless seconds passed and then they reappeared, struggling to stay afloat and clinging on to the bags stuffed full of dollars. Fernandísimo shouted to them:

— Such a shame, children. You decided to be poor and lose your lives.

Then, excited, that is to say with me in his heart, he began to sing and dance a bright and cheerful tune, full of lively rhythms and melodies of beautiful worlds.

— Come on, Arab. You dance too and throw off your rags.

And the two men, while they danced and sang, took off their clothes, the turban flying into the air, shoes into the water onto the heads of Antonieta and Ricardo, shirts, underpants, t-shirts, socks, watches, rings, necklaces, and anything else that could be removed. Everything went into the air or the water.

Fred, the police officer, couldn't stop being a cop even though he was enjoying the scene.

— Gentlemen, it's against morality and good manners to undress on a public thoroughfare.

And Fernandísimo, more cheerful than ever, replied:

— What pretentious and arrogant fool said that? God sent us here as we are now. Do you work for God or for the government?

Fred hesitated. He'd never thought of it that way.

— But, gentlemen, I'll have to...

The policeman was unable to finish what he was saying. Fernandísimo, Mr. Bob and Tarud Arab, as naked as newborn babies, began running across the bridge like a gust of wind. The dog barked exultantly and both men sang like children, free and crazy like birds of paradise. The policeman scratched his head as he watched them gallop away. But what Fred didn't see was that the trio suddenly took a magical leap and their bodies began to rise toward the sky and the wonderful lights of the Manhattan night. From on high they admired that well crafted beauty, so carefully and exquisitely produced, but with the lightness of their new state they felt that beauty was in exchange for something, that the city was sinking the island with the tremendous burden of such vain endeavor, the senseless bustle with so much created interest, with this painful burden of collective and individual dramas, with all that show business for just a few dollars more, with banks and their one-sided interests, with Wall Street deals, with the ignominious weight of the discriminations and arguments or the great invented conflicts, fabricated by those who believe that man has to be a slave of man. It is not the Americans who have made Manhattan a burden that submerges the pristine islet into the river on which it lies, but simply men. And as they rose higher and higher, they saw the lights of many cities around the world, and they saw that the burden was the same everywhere and that unnecessary weight was sinking the Earth everywhere. They also saw Antonieta and Ricardo swimming desperately, trying to salvage the heavy bags of treasure. We'll leave them there for a while. Let's be fair, let's respect their freedom to decide.

And when they passed over the Statue of Liberty, Fernandísimo told his flight companions:

— That great lady holding up the torch not only tells us that men have the right to be happy and free from the tyrannical desires of other men, but to be above all the tyranny we exercise over ourselves. She tells us to free ourselves from the teachings of the world and open our minds and our hearts to respect and love. Freedom is to renounce the terrible human being who keeps us tied to our miserable pursuits and selfishness.

— Beautiful words —said a light and happy Tarud Arab as he flew higher.

— The wisest I've ever heard —Mr. Bob barked happily.

And so they kept rising, beyond the stars, closer and closer to here. The last thing they saw from the Earth way below was the glow of the torch as a symbol of hope to let mankind know that there is a future in which someday elephants will not have elephant brains and nor will humans have the brains of men.

It's said that some sailors, who were navigating New York Bay in the middle of the night at the time that those three wise men were passing close by the Statue of Liberty, may have seen, for the first time in their lives, how the Great Lady with the Torch at the entrance to New York may have smiled liked a contented goddess. I'm telling you, so you know it's true.

END

New Jersey, Union City, July 18, 2016 (1:25 p.m.)

Printed in the United States
By Bookmasters